Book One

Linda Joy Singleton

Albert Whitman & Company
Chicago, Illinois

Library of Congress Cataloging-in-Publication data
is on file with the publisher.

Text copyright © 2015 by Linda Joy Singleton
Cover illustration copyright © 2015 by Kristi Valiant
Interior illustrations and hand lettering by Jordan Kost
Published in 2015 by Albert Whitman & Company
ISBN 978-0-8075-1376-7

Printed in China.
10 9 8 7 6 5 4 3 2 1 NP 20 19 18 17 16 15 14

Design by Jordan Kost and Ellen Kokontis

For more information about Albert Whitman & Company,
visit our web site at www.albertwhitman.com.

To Lori Welch, who formed the real
Curious Cat Spy Club with me when we were kids

Contents

Chapter 1: Dumped   1

Chapter 2: Alley Cats   11

Chapter 3: Mews and Clues   21

Chapter 4: Shack Attack   29

Chapter 5: The Zorse's Tale   37

Chapter 6: Kelsey the Spy   51

Chapter 7: Secret Friends   59

Chapter 8: A Fishy Clue   67

Chapter 9: Mis-Stake-Out   75

Chapter 10: Dog Gone   85

Chapter 11: Bird-Drone Blast-Off   91

Chapter 12: Clue or Coincidence?   105

Chapter 13: Wild Times at Wild Oaks   119

Chapter 14: Lost and Found   127

Chapter 15: Secrets and Lies   135

Chapter 16: Grave Suspicions   145

Chapter 17: Spies and Lies   151

Chapter 18: Accusations   157

Chapter 19: Cat-Tastrophe   167

Chapter 20: Follow That Pet-Napper!   175

Chapter 21: Mysterious Mama Cat   185

Chapter 22: What Kelsey Found   195

Chapter 23: Guilty and Innocent   205

Chapter 24: Caged   213

Chapter 25: Rescue   217

Chapter 26: Interrogated   225

Chapter 27: A Little Bit of Justice   231

- Chapter 1 -
Dumped

What's black and white and runs through traffic?

A runaway zebra.

This isn't a joke—it's really happening!

I'm waiting at the crosswalk and almost stumble off the curb when black-and-white stripes gallop through a red light. Cars honk, tires screech and someone screams. I jump away from the curb with a gasp.

What's a zebra doing on Pleasant Street?

"Stop that zorse!" a girl shouts, her pink-streaked hair flying behind her like a tail as she chases after the galloping beast.

I'm not sure if I'm more shocked to see a runaway zebra or to recognize the girl from Helen Corning

Middle School. Becca Morales sits in front of me in science so I stare at the back of her head Monday through Friday, quietly wishing she'd turn around to talk to me. I love how the pink streaks shimmer in her black hair so much that once I pink-streaked my golden-brown hair. But no one even noticed.

"Stop that zorse!" Becca shouts again.

I look around, hoping someone will help her. But people are diving off the sidewalk into stores, rushing to safety. The zebra...or *zorse*...weaves wildly through traffic, skidding to avoid a truck. He whinnies, rears up, and runs toward the sidewalk where I'm standing.

Clutching my backpack with its sweet-smelling bag inside, I think about running for safety too. I could duck into O'Hara Realty or hide behind a large postal box. But when I hear Becca's panicked shouts, I remember when my pen ran out of ink and she turned around with a generous smile and offered me her glitter-tipped pink pen. And she let me keep it.

I get an idea and quickly unzip my backpack. As I reach inside and grab a paper bag, I hear hooves clattering toward me.

"Stop!" I yell, which really doesn't do much to slow the zorse.

Becca is yelling too. "Kelsey! Get out of the way!"

I should take cover but instead I stand there, grinning. Becca Morales, the nicest and most liked girl at school, remembers my name. Wow.

The zorse suddenly stops a few feet from me, eyes wide and wild as cars honk and swerve into a jumbled traffic jam. Before he can bolt again, I reach into the paper bag and then plunge into the street with my hand held out to the trembling animal.

"Here, zorsey," I yell over the commotion, but gentle and soothing, like when our dog, Handsome, used to freak out during storms and hide in the closet. That was before we moved into a no-pets apartment and Handsome moved in with Gran Nola.

"Come and get the yummy treat," I singsong, hoping the zorse likes my dad's homemade oatmeal-carrot cookies. Up close to this amazing creature, I admire his long, curly lashes. His eyes are gorgeous! Shiny, black, and intelligent—like if he could talk he'd have fabulous stories to tell.

The zorse blinks at me then looks at the cookies in my palm. He sniffs, lips the cookies, and then my hand is empty. When I look up, Becca is snapping a rope to the zorse's halter. She leads him off the sidewalk to a secluded corner between two shops, and I follow.

Holding the rope firmly, Becca bends over to catch her breath. She isn't even sweating. Though I sure am! She looks chic in a leopard-print blouse over boot-cut black jeans. Animal prints are like her trademark, probably because her family lives on an animal sanctuary. Sometimes in class I peek over her shoulder while she's showing cool animal photos to her friends.

"That was scary!" Becca shudders. "I thought Zed would be roadkill."

"He's safe now." I feed Zed another cookie, his moist lips tickling my palm.

"Luckily no one was hurt. You were really brave," Becca says gratefully. "Thanks, Kelsey."

I feel my cheeks go warm. I don't know what to say. Should I thank her for thanking me? I don't hang out with other kids much, except my older brother Kyle and my sisters Kenya and Kiana. Being the youngest means shouting to be heard or keeping quiet. I've gotten so good at listening that I taught myself to lip-read. But Becca is waiting for me to say something, and for the first time ever, silence feels awkward.

Around us, traffic resumes, although a few drivers slow to stare at us. I mean, it's not every day you see a zorse in downtown Sun Flower.

I'm curious too and study the bizarre animal. Stockier than a horse, Zed has a shiny black head with a silky dark mane waving down to a black-and-white body and sturdy legs striped like vanilla-licorice candy canes.

"He's a gorgeous animal," Becca says, offering me an encouraging smile in the same generous way she once offered me a pink pen.

"What is he?" I ask puzzled. "A zebra or a horse?"

"Both!" Becca laughs and pats Zed fondly on the neck. "This amazing creature is part horse and part zebra. Very rare."

"Why isn't he in a zoo?"

"He's domesticated, not wild."

"He sure looked wild running through traffic."

"Yeah." Becca winces. "He kicks up a fuss when he has to ride in a trailer so I told Mom I'd walk him to the vet. Bad idea. I should have known better than to take him on a major street."

"You call this street *major*?" Sun Flower is a suburban town with miles of housing developments but only three blocks residents fondly call "downtown."

"Any street with noise is major for Zed," Becca answers. "He spooked when a truck horn blasted. He's calm now. See how he eats from your hand without biting? He's such a sweetheart—it's a crime how he was treated."

"Crime?" The word piques my interest and makes me think of my bookshelf collection of spy novels and mysteries.

"Most of the animals we care for at Wild Oaks were mistreated. Zed has an interesting history," Becca says with a mysterious glint in her dark-cocoa eyes. "But there's no time to tell you. Zed is late for his check-up."

"I'm late too." I frown at the paper bag I'm holding.

"For what?"

"Delivering cookies to Veteran's Hall. My dad volunteers there. Cookies, cakes, breads—you name it, he bakes it." I don't add that Dad has lots of time for volunteer work since Café Belmond closed and he lost his job. "Dad asked me to deliver the cookies, only…" I sigh and lift up the half-empty bag. "Zed ate most of them."

Zed whinnies at the sound of his name and lunges for the bag. I jump back but not fast enough. His large teeth crunch down, snatching the bag out of my hands. Cookies fly like golden Frisbees, one smacking my forehead.

"NO, ZED!" Becca yanks his rope. The bag rips, cookies spilling to the pavement, crumbling into pieces.

"Drats. Now they're *all* gone." I wipe crumbs from my forehead and stare in dismay at the splattered cookies. "Dad spent hours baking those. I am sooo in trouble when I get home."

"How much trouble?" Becca bites her lower lip like she really cares. "When I mess up, my parents punish me by taking away my cell phone."

"Mine won't do that to me," I say honestly. As the youngest in a family where money is scarce, I don't have a cell phone.

"What will they do to you?"

"Give me disgusting chores like scrubbing toilets." I don't want to sound pathetic so I add jokingly, "Can I move in with you for a while?"

"Sure, but you'll have to share a bed with two dogs and a goat. And my goat snores."

I'm sure she's joking too, but she doesn't laugh.

"I'm really sorry, Kelsey." Becca puts her hand on my shoulder. "I won't let you get in trouble for something that was my fault. You helped me, so I'll help you. After I drop Zed off at the vet, I'll go with you to your house and explain how you rescued Zed and prevented car crashes and probably saved lives too. I'll say that you don't deserve to be punished—you deserve a medal for bravery."

I laugh. "My parents won't believe you...but it might help."

So I go with her.

Zed follows nicely, no more escape attempts.

We walk a few blocks, then Becca gasps and stops abruptly like she's slammed into an invisible wall.

"Don't let him see me!" Becca spins around and ducks behind Zed.

"Who?" I follow her gaze but don't see anyone until a red flash catches my eye. A boy with a fiery red ponytail stands by a corner, his hands in the pockets of his baggy jeans. I'd recognize that blazing-red-means-trouble hair anywhere—and I duck behind the zorse too.

Burton Skeet is a popular kid with a pretty face but ugly attitude. Girls seem to like him, which puzzles me because he's pure meanness. I've seen him cram small kids into lockers or toss them into basketball hoops. Since I'm on the short side, I stay out of his way. But I heard he has a major crush on Becca, so why is she avoiding him?

"We're taking a short cut!" Becca yanks my arm and Zed's rope toward an alley.

"Why? I thought you and Skeet were friends."

"He thinks so." She swerves around a decaying car tire. "Can we not talk about him, please?"

I nod. Not talking is easy. Cutting through the alley is hard—especially if you have a nose and can smell the stinky sewage and rotting food. I don't complain, though, because my brain buzzes with questions. Why is Becca avoiding Skeet? Does she really share a room with a snoring goat? And what is Zed's mysterious history?

We're almost through the alley, which is a relief. The smell alone is enough to knock over a herd of zorses. And it's worse as we near a huge metal dumpster surrounded by gross litter. Are those white sticks actually bones?

Becca doesn't seem to mind though she carefully steps over the bones. Zed's hooves clatter, echoing off the tall buildings on each side of us. I hurry to keep up until I hear a cry from inside the dumpster.

I stop to listen. Nothing…Wait…what was that? Shutting out sounds of Becca, Zed, and nearby traffic, I focus my hearing like it's my secret weapon. There it is again—faint crying sounds.

Definitely coming from the dumpster. Something alive. A homeless person? Rats? (I imagine blood-thirsty, fanged monster rats.) Shivers crawl up my skin. I am so out of here.

I turn to run fast and far from this creepy alley but I only get a few feet before I stop again. I clearly hear mewing. Not just one mew but a chorus of shrill, scared mews—trapped inside the dumpster.

Kittens.

- Chapter 2 -
Alley Cats

"Becca!" I shout as I run toward the sound of crying kittens.

"What?" she calls from farther down the alley.

"Get over here! Now!"

My heart is racing faster than my feet as I approach the dumpster. It's almost as tall as me. (Which isn't saying much since I'm not quite five feet.) I hear footsteps and hooves coming closer. But I don't wait for Becca because the kittens are mewing desperately. They need help *now*.

Broken glass crunches under my sneakers as I lean against the dumpster, grabbing the lid with both hands. I summon all my strength and push up. But the metal lid is so heavy and I'm not strong enough.

"What are you doing?" Becca ties Zed's rope to a pipe sticking out from a building and hurries over to me.

"Help me lift the lid!"

"Are you nuts? Why would anyone want to get inside that stinky thing?"

"To rescue the kittens trapped in there!" I shove harder but it's like I'm an ant trying to lift a truck. The lid won't budge.

"Kittens?" Becca tosses her tangled dark curls from her eyes as she stares in horror at the dumpster.

"I hear them mewing!" I cry. "Help me get them out!"

Together we heave and shove at the lid. The left side lifts an inch but the right side has a smashed-in corner and won't budge. Still, we keep trying, all the time my heart breaking at the sound of kitten cries. Can they breathe? Are they smothering in garbage? Are they injured? And the biggest question—who could be so cruel to dump kittens in the garbage?

"We're not strong enough," Becca says, wincing as she examines her scraped palms.

"They'll die if we don't free them! We can't give up!"

"Did I say I was giving up? No way." Becca purses her plum-frosted lips in determination. "But we need help."

I look up and down the alley and shake my head. "There's no one here to help."

"But there's a basketball court around the corner where some hoop players I know practice most Saturdays. If we're lucky they'll all be there and we'll have a whole team to help."

Of course jocks would want to help Becca. She has a smile that makes you feel good inside, and people just naturally like her. I'm not unpopular—not like Greta Ying who has a short fuse and gets into fights or geeky Leo Polanski who mumbles to himself and writes on a tablet while he eats lunch alone. Kids just don't notice me, which is a good thing since I want to be a spy someday.

"Stay here with Zed," Becca says as she turns to leave. "I'll bring back some muscle."

It's creepy being alone in a shadowy alley but I'm more afraid for the poor trapped kittens. Their tiny mews break my heart yet give me hope. They're still alive...for now. Is it my imagination or have their mews grown softer?

"Stay strong, little ones," I whisper into the cracked-open corner of the dumpster lid. "Don't worry. Everything will be okay."

That's what Dad said to us after he lost his job. "Everything will be okay." Only everything sucked. We lost our wonderful two-story house with the half-acre backyard. A new family lives there now. I rode past on my bike once and saw a smiling mother beneath my favorite oak tree, pushing a toddler in my rope-swing. I haven't ridden past there again.

But the worst was giving up our dog. I call Handsome a "Golden Whip" since he's a golden retriever–whippet mix. He's so high energy he'd ping off the walls if our apartment allowed pets. Still, the no-pets rule really sucks. Sure, I can still see Handsome when I visit Gran Nola, but it's not the same. I miss his warm body curled up against me at night and his sweet doggie kisses.

Ever since the move I've been troubled by reoccurring dreams. You'd think I'd dream about Handsome coming back to us. But no, these dreams are all about cats. A crying cat in the night wakes me, so I climb out of bed to look out the window. Yellow-gold eyes stare at me through the glass—a skinny stray cat with fluffy honey-orange fur. His long whiskers tickle as I carry him into my room. I give him food. I let him sleep on a pillow on my bed. And when I cuddle him, he purrs contentedly. In my dream my parents are more understanding than in real life and they let me keep him. He'll be my cat forever and sleep with me every night. Then my door opens and the apartment manager, a sorrow-eyed widow named Mrs. Bledsoe, snatches the cat from my arms. I run after her, crying for my cat...and that's usually when I wake up.

But my dreams never included a filthy, littered, stinky alley. I hear a whinny and go over to Zed and pet him and tell him to be patient. Then I return to the dumpster and try pushing the lid again. I take a break to catch my breath, listening for more mewing. The dumpster is deathly quiet. No rustling. No mews. Silence.

"Please be alive," I whisper into the small crack.

It seems like hours but it's probably only ten minutes before Becca returns. I see someone hurrying behind her and my heart soars with hope—until I recognize the guy. Not a tall, muscular basketball player. The total opposite.

OMG! Leo Polanski?

Why in the world would Becca bring *him* for heavy lifting? He's almost as short as me and tapping on a tablet seems to be his only sport.

"Look who I found, Kelsey," Becca says, like she's delivering a present all wrapped and shiny with ribbons.

I don't know what to say. Leo seems nice enough, but he's useless. He's not even wearing normal clothes. I mean, who wears formal slacks with a black vest over a white long-sleeved buttoned shirt on a Saturday morning?

"Um...hi, Leo," I say with zero enthusiasm.

"Wow. You know my name!" His huge grin is a little lopsided but kind of sweet in an eager-puppy way.

I glance away guiltily. I only know his name because I've overheard kids mocking him with mean names. Loser Leo and Leo-Nerdo. I don't want to be a mean kid even in my thoughts. But I can't help feeling disappointed. We need someone with the strength of a super hero, not a wimpy sidekick.

"Leo knows how to get the kittens out," Becca says confidently.

I'm doubtful but with three of us pushing we have a better chance of opening the lid. I ignore the stinging pain in my palms and resume the lifting position.

But Leo comes over and nudges me out of the way. "According to my calculations, you're doing it all wrong," he says.

"Oh?" I lift my brows, annoyed. "I suppose you can open it all by yourself."

"Actually, I can," he says matter-of-factly. "If you'll move aside..."

How quickly the eager puppy turns into a bossy bulldog! His tablet sticks up from his back pocket, and I remember all the times I felt sorry for him, mumbling and tapping alone during lunch. I even considered sitting with him, asking what he's writing. But I no longer feel guilty for ignoring him. He's the rudest guy I've ever met, bossing me around while those poor kittens are running out of time.

"Let's all push together," I say stubbornly. "You're not strong enough."

"I'm strong of mind if not body."

"It'll take brawn, not brains, to un-jam that stuck corner." I point to the lid.

"Criticizing me is counteractive." Leo frowns. "I figured you were the quiet type, but clearly you talk too much. You're wasting my time."

"Wasting *your* time!" My hands clench into fists that would love to smack the know-it-all look off his face.

"Kelsey, give him a chance." Becca hurries over and whispers in my ear. "He was the only one at the basketball court. He wasn't even playing—just tapping on his tablet. He wants to help so let him."

Wanting and actually doing aren't the same thing. But I won't argue with Becca. After Leo fails miserably I'll go find a guy with muscles.

I expect Leo to try to lift the lid like we did. But he paces back and forth, tilting his blond head and rubbing his chin like he's concentrating hard or hoping for chin hair. He steps away from the dumpster, bends down, and sorts through random trash. He picks up bones (chicken? steak? human?) and tosses them down, the sound brittle and sharp, startling Zed.

"Why are you playing with bones instead of freeing the kittens?" I demand.

"Playing?" He huffs indignantly. "I've evaluated the situation and am now proceeding toward a solution which requires a sturdy wedge to prop open this corner." He gestures to the unjammed side of the lid then shoves in a small piece of wood.

"We already tried to push that corner. It's the other side that's stuck. It'll take someone really strong to lift it." My tone clearly says, "Not you."

He glares at me then stomps across the alley to sort through a pile of rusty metal pipes. He chooses a long pipe, wielding it like he's pretending to be a knight in a role playing game. Seriously? Kittens may be dying and he's larping?

I've had enough of Leo's weirdness and turn to Becca. "Come on, we have to find someone who—"

A sharp metallic sound stops me. I whirl around to see Leo aim the long steel pipe at the un-jammed corner of the dumpster lid. He shoves the front of the pipe into the small opening, metal grinding, so that the end of the pipe sticks up into the air over Leo's head. Stepping back, Leo reaches high with both hands to grasp the end of the pipe. He pulls down hard with all his body weight, his feet lifting off the ground. The dumpster makes a grinding sound. Then, astonishingly, the lid pops open.

"Basic physics," Leo says, pulling out a handkerchief from his vest pocket and wiping his hands. "No brawn required."

"You did it!" Becca jumps excitedly.

"It was a simple matter of leverage." Leo looks directly at me. "I'm used to being underestimated."

"I've never been so glad to be wrong in my life," I admit, rushing over to the dumpster.

My heart thumps as I peer into the smelly pit of discarded food, papers, cartons, clothes, and plastic bags. No kittens. But they have to be here! I carefully lift gross stuff, searching desperately. Becca and Leo search too. I focus all my energy on listening, praying for a whisper of kitten mews.

Then I hear something. It's so faint, so feeble, that I think I'm imagining the sound. But then I hear it again.

"Over there!" I shout, pointing to a back corner of the dumpster.

Leo, in his nice slacks and vest, grips the edge of the dumpster and pulls himself up and then balances on his stomach, reaching over to pull out the wiggling plastic bag. He carries the bag to the ground and gently rips it open.

Tiny balls of fur peek out.

Three kitties...alive!

- Chapter 3 -
Mews and Clues

I'm overwhelmed with joy, relief, and love. But I'm angry too—at the horrible person who trapped helpless kittens in a plastic bag then dumped them like trash.

I reach for the orange kitty just as Becca scoops up the black kitten and Leo goes for the calico.

"Most calico cats are females, you know," Leo says matter-of-factly but his expression is all mushy with kitty love as he cuddles the kitten.

"Mine is midnight black except for white feet like snowy boots. And it's a"—Becca lifts up the kitten's tail—"a male."

"Kelsey's kitten is male too," Leo adds without even looking.

"How do you know?" I ask.

"The color of a cat's coat is determined by genes in the X chromosome. Only one in twenty-seven orange cats are female."

I check my kitten then grin smugly. "Not a male. Guess mine is a special one."

"All the kittens are special," Becca says, quickly stepping in between us. "My little guy is so tiny he fits inside my hand. He's not skinny so they haven't been away from their mother long."

"How old do you think they are?" I ask.

"Not very old." When Becca bends closer to study the kitten, it paws at her dangling black curls. "About five weeks."

"I wonder what happened to their mother," I say, petting the orange kitten.

Leo shakes his head. "Nothing good."

"Yeah." Becca blows out a heavy sigh. "At least the kittens are safe."

Safe, I think gratefully, tickling behind the kitten's furry orange ears. I love how soft and perfect she feels in my hands; like she's meant to be there. Purring, she rubs her silky fur against my fingers. I get this strange feeling because holding an orange kitty reminds me of my cat dream. Though this kitten isn't as fluffy and she has a stubby tail.

If only I could keep her…

Swallowing hard, I look at Becca. "Our apartment doesn't allow pets. But you live on an animal sanctuary so you can take them home."

I'm surprised when she shakes her head. "Mom says no more animals—especially cats since we're already fostering six."

"I'm only allowed to have fish," Leo adds, frowning. "My father suffers from pet allergies."

"Drats. There's nowhere else for them to go— except the county shelter," I say sadly. "At least the shelter will find them good homes."

"Um…that won't work." Becca shifts uneasily. "Mom volunteers for the Humane Society and says all the shelter cages are full and they're low on funds. If animals aren't adopted quickly, it's a death sentence."

"No!" I cry, hugging the kitten closer. "I won't let my kitten die!"

"Me neither," Leo says firmly.

Becca nods, close to tears.

We share a worried look as we each hold a kitten. We don't know each other well, and we're very different, but I know we're all thinking the same thing. We have to save our kittens.

After a long silence Becca snaps her fingers. "I have an idea."

"What?" Leo and I ask eagerly.

"The Humane Society Fund-Raiser Fair is next month. It's fun and helps shelter animals get adopted. Afterward we'll have room for more animals at Wild Oaks and I know Mom will let me foster the kittens. We just have to find a safe place for them until the fund-raiser."

"What kind of safe place?" Leo asks, rubbing his chin.

"Well..." Becca hesitates, looking hopefully at us. "If you don't mind mucking through mud and scratchy weeds, I know a place."

"Bring on the mud," I say.

"Weeds can't stop me." Leo whips his hand like he's slicing through a jungle. "Where is it?"

"In the woods at the back of our property, there's an old shack—we call it the Skunk Shack because it used to quarantine sick or smelly animals. But it's been abandoned forever." She bites her lower lip, gazing down at the kitten she's cuddling. "So what do you think?"

"Sounds great! I won't worry about the kittens if they're with you." I smile but inside I'm sad because I don't want to give up my adorable orange honey. Honey, that's what I'd name her if I could keep her. It's only been a few minutes since we met, but I'm completely, totally in love.

Leo is nodding too, but he looks just as sad as I feel. It must be hard to have a parent allergic to animals. At least I can hope to move to a house again where I can have pets. But poor Leo is stuck without pets until he's an adult. And I can tell he's in love with his calico too.

"But I can't do it alone," Becca says firmly. "I need you both to help. You can start by taking the kittens to the Skunk Shack while I take Zed to the vet. Then I'll join you there."

I don't remind her that she offered to come to my house and explain how Zed ate Dad's missing cookies. Getting the kittens to a safe place is more important. I don't mind scrubbing toilets much anyway.

"There's a back gate so you can come and go without anyone knowing," Becca adds. "We'll have to clean the Skunk Shack and make a feeding schedule. And we'll need kitten supplies, so we'll need to figure out expenses. Are you okay with that?"

I nod, willing to do anything for the kittens.

Becca and I turn to Leo, waiting for his answer. He's tilting his blond head, looking serious, and I think he's going to refuse. But again I'm wrong about him.

"Great plan. But I want to do more," he finally says. "First I need to tell you something I've never told anyone else. My therapist says I need to work on my social skills, that I spend too much time sketching robot designs. I understand electronic components, wires, connectors, and motors better than people. Most kids think I'm weird or a loser."

Becca and I share a guilty look.

"I've tried to do normal things like play soccer and baseball but I don't work well in groups," Leo admits, stroking his kitten's tummy. "My team ends up hating me. But there's one thing I've always wanted."

"What?" Becca and I ask at the same time.

"To belong to a club," he says. "Only nothing interested me—until now. What we're doing here is important. We have all the elements for a club. A goal to help these kittens, three members, and a secret clubhouse."

"I guess we do," Becca says, smiling. "A cat rescue club."

"We'll need a better club name—but I'll work on it," Leo says.

"A club would be cool," I agree. I pause as something occurs to me. "But our goal shouldn't only be to help our kittens."

"What do you mean?" Becca arches a dark brow curiously.

"I want to find the monster that left these kittens in a dumpster to die. And I already have my first clue." I reach for the plastic bag the kittens were trapped inside. I'd noticed something when Leo ripped into the bag. I dig inside the bag and pull out a crumpled slip of paper. "A store receipt."

Leo bends over for a closer look. "It's from Dalton's Pet Supply for $28.27 dated two days ago."

"Dumping animals is cruel and illegal." I grit my teeth with determination. "I'm going to track down the horrible person who tried to kill these sweet kittens."

"Me too," Leo says.

"Me three." Becca grins. "We're in a club now. Let's solve this mystery. Together."

- Chapter 4 -
Shack Attack

While Becca takes Zed to his late vet appointment, Leo and I head for the Skunk Shack.

"Are you sure you know the way?" I ask Leo, who is holding the map Becca sketched for us. He's taken the lead like he knows exactly where we're going—which I seriously doubt.

"Trust me—I'll get us there. I don't even need this." He folds Becca's map into a perfect square and tucks it into his pocket.

"Why'd you do that? We'll never find the shack without a map."

"This is more precise." He whips a cell phone from his pocket. It looks like the latest model, sleek, silver, and small. I'm a little envious—but I don't tell Leo.

I shrug like a fancy phone is no big deal. "Calling someone for directions?"

"Not necessary." He taps a few buttons and a map flashes onto the tiny screen. "The red dot is our location and the blue dot is our destination."

I squint at the flashing dots. "It doesn't look too far."

"According to my calculations, it's one point six miles."

"Huh?" I blink. "You mean like almost two miles?"

"Almost is not a unit of distance. And it's closer to a mile and a half."

I sigh. I can deal with the long walk, but can I deal with Leo and his annoying calculations? Doubtful.

Still, I follow.

While Leo navigates with his phone, I carry the kittens in a sports cap from my backpack. Our tiny fur babies are so cute curled together.

Funny how I already think of the kittens as ours. Leo's curious green-eyed calico mews a lot; Becca's sweet black kitten sleeps peacefully; and my darling orange Honey stares up at me with trusting golden-eyes, purring like she knows I'll keep her safe.

We turn on Wild Road, leaving behind city lights and traffic. Hills roll and curve and rise into towering trees. I inhale the woodsy scent of pines, enjoying the sound of wind whooshing through branches. But after about a mile of climbing uphill, I'm breathing hard and the wind stings my face.

, Finally Leo stops in front of a metal gate. "We're here!" he announces.

I look past the gate into a shadowy forest then point to a sign fixed on the gate. "No trespassing," I read. An ominous shiver zaps me.

"Becca invited us, so we aren't trespassers. See, the gate isn't even locked." Leo lifts a latch and gestures for me to follow him through the gate.

I hesitate, staring into a murky maze of trees. I don't see any roads or buildings. What if we run into a bear or a mountain lion? What if we get lost and never find our way out? My stomach jumps nervously. I'm not so sure this is a good idea. But I remind myself I'm doing this for the kittens.

The gate clangs shut behind us.

Leo strides ahead, navigating with the compass app on his phone. He pushes through bushes until he finds a trail winding along a narrow stream. Although it hasn't rained in a week, the grass is damp and my sneakers slosh in muddy weeds. Prickly bushes snag my hair and clothes as we walk deeper into the woods. The ground dips then rises, and I stumble over a rotting log.

"Leo!" I cry out as the cap flies from my hands.

Quick as a breath, Leo lunges and catches the cap of kittens.

I'm not so lucky though and land smack on muddy ground. My knee stings where there's now a hole in my favorite pair of jeans. I try to stand but slip and slide into the mud.

"You could offer to help." I hold up a mud-splattered hand.

"I am helping. I saved the kittens." Leo looks at me critically. "You're too messy to touch the kittens so I'll carry them to the shack."

"Thanks," I say, but he totally misses my sarcasm. I glare at him as I push myself out of the mud.

He takes off in the lead again, his phone app guiding the way. We're so deep in the woods now that trees form a leafy umbrella shutting out the sky. I tense whenever I hear rustling or fluttering in the bushes. Are wild animals lurking, ready to attack? When we step out of the trees into a marshy meadow of waving green grass, I'm so relieved.

"According to my calculations, the shack should be here," Leo says, gesturing to the meadow.

I shake my head. "Well, it's not."

He scrunches his forehead as he looks down at his phone. "The directional app can't be wrong."

"Guess it wasn't precise enough." With a roll of my eyes, I pluck Becca's map from his pocket. "I prefer a real map."

"Those scribbles won't help," Leo scoffs.

I unfold the map. The symbols and directions are like clues and I'm good at figuring out clues in mystery novels. I trace my finger along a line. That's the road we walked on. My finger trails to a tiny square—the gate with the no-trespassing sign. The squiggly lines must be the meadow where we're standing right now. But what do the triangle, circle, and letter Y mean? Maybe the circle is the small pond across the meadow. Beyond it is a pointy rock—like a triangle. Above the rock is a Y-shaped tree. I stare past the tree into dense brush and see a glassy glint. A window!

With a triumphant grin, I lead smarty-pants Leo to the Skunk Shack.

The shack is covered in vines, cobwebs, and bird droppings. And it stinks.

Apparently the roof is a favorite roosting spot for birds. I step in white goo and scuff my shoe to get it off but it only smears. Yuck.

Leo sets down the sleeping kittens, carefully placing his jacket around the cap so they'll stay warm. He rolls up his white shirt sleeves and we get to work tackling the vines. It's like a game of tug of war. Team Kittens against the Sticky Vines. It's a tough battle but ultimately Team Kittens triumphs.

•We rip off the vines, yank the door open—and fluttering wings whoosh out of the shack.

Shrieking, I stumble backward. I wave my hands over my head to ward off bird bombs. But the birds have all flown away.

Cautiously, I take a step into the shack.

"Ewww!" There's broken furniture, gooey messes across a dirty floor, and feathers everywhere—even in the cobwebs. "It's filthy!"

"It's perfect," Leo says, smiling.

"Perfect for birds," I retort.

"Perfect for a clubhouse."

I plug my nose. "I've never seen so much bird poop and cobwebs."

"It just needs a little cleaning," he insists.

"A little!" I shake my head, so disappointed I could cry. I'd been excited about having a secret place to keep our kittens. But this shack is a shambles of feathers, filth, and bird goo. We can't leave the kittens here.

Leo just grins wider. "You should see our house— it's all white. Walls, carpets, even the furniture. If I sneeze, Mom sprays disinfectant all over—even on me. She *never* lets me get dirty. Fixing up this shack is going to be fun."

I open my mouth to tell him what I think of his idea of fun when a branch snaps outside the shack.

"What was *that*?" I whisper.

"Don't know," Leo whispers back.

Another branch snaps—closer this time.

We stare past the open door. His eyes are wide, and I'm sure mine are even wider.

Something is out there.

Something big enough to snap branches.

What if it's a coyote, a cougar, or a bear?

I lunge forward to slam the door—but stop as a terrible thought hits me.

The kittens are still outside.

Chapter 5

The Zorse's Tale

Before I can say anything to Leo, I hear a shout.

"Kelsey! Leo! Where are you?"

I jerk open the door and run outside. "Becca!" I exclaim.

I'm so relieved to see her instead of a kid-hungry bear that I want to hug her. But her arms are full as she lifts a huge cardboard box from a red wagon.

"Whew!" Becca sets the box down in front of the shack and wipes sweat from her brow. "My house isn't far—just over that hill—but pulling a wagon made it feel like miles." She reaches for her sleepy black kitten. "Why'd you leave the kittens out here?"

"The shack is creepy," I say with a shudder.

"Ignore the scaredy-cat—and I don't mean the kittens." Leo scoops up his calico. "There's nothing wrong with the shack. It's perfect for a clubhouse."

"It's stinky and gross." I pluck a feather off my shoe.

"Cleaning will fix it up," Leo insists.

"I love your positive attitude, Leo," Becca says, smiling.

Does that mean she thinks I have a bad attitude? Suddenly it feels like Leo and I are in a competition for Becca's approval. And he's winning. So even though I'm covered in mud and bird poop, I force a smile. "I guess it's not that bad. I mean, it *is* a cool shack...or it will be when it's clean."

"Just what I hoped you would say." Becca gestures to the huge box. "Look what I brought."

Inside the box are a broom and a mop. I never knew I could be so excited by cleaning supplies. But I'm even more excited by what I find at the bottom of the box.

"Yay! Cat food!" I lift up a flat of cans. "And litter, a litter box, and an adorable fuzzy kitty bed. Becca, how did you get it all?"

"From my cousin Danielle—she's a vet tech."

"You told her about our kittens?" Leo looks shocked.

"I only told her I needed kitten supplies for a secret project. I didn't say anything about our club. She's cool and didn't ask questions. She went to a storage room and gave me all the cat supplies." Becca gestures to the box. "Vets get lots of free samples. Then Danielle drove me and Zed home— where I got all the cleaning stuff. Can you both stay to help clean the shack?"

"Sure," I answer. My parents will think I went to the library after I dropped off the cookies... which I didn't do. But I'll deal with that problem when I get home.

"I can stay all day," Leo adds, petting the calico kitten curled in his arms. "My parents work late, even on weekends."

"So let's get started. Lunch first—for the kitties." Becca pops open a tin of cat food. "I hope they're weaned or we'll have to bottle-feed."

Honey leaps to the opened can and the other kittens scamper to join her. "They *definitely* know how to eat," I say. "Cute little chowhounds."

"Cats are not hounds," Leo objects.

Becca and I just laugh.

Then we get busy fixing up the shack.

I sweep away trash until my arms feel like they'll fall off. Becca scrubs the only window. Leo salvages the best pieces of furniture. There are four chairs (one is missing a leg); a banged-up wood table; a cabinet with a door that won't close; and a grandfather clock that looks older than my actual grandfather with more broken parts than working ones.

"What's a giant clock doing in an old shack?" I ask Becca.

"Don't know." She shrugs. "It was here when we bought the property. My parents thought someone would come back for it only no one ever did so they left it here."

Another puzzle for me to solve, I think. That makes three mysteries:

How did the zorse end up on Wild Oaks Animal Sanctuary?

Why was the grandfather clock left in the shack?

Who tossed the kittens into the dumpster?

Naturally Leo, the robot-gadget geek, falls in love with the clock. But we forbid him to touch it until we're done cleaning.

An hour later, the shack is transformed. No dirt or feathers or cobwebs. And the window is so clear it's almost invisible, like I could reach my hand through it and grab a pine branch.

We're filthy and exhausted but grinning. Working hard never felt so good.

"Here's our reward," Becca announces, grabbing a bag I hadn't noticed from her box. She lifts out chips and drinks, and we sit in now-clean chairs at the slanted table.

This is my chance to get some answers.

"So what's the story with Zed?" I ask, my chair wobbling a little as I lean toward Becca. "You said he had an interesting past."

"He sure does!" Becca rips open the bag of corn chips, her dark eyes shining. "Most animals come to Wild Oaks Animal Sanctuary because they've been mistreated. Starved, beaten, abandoned... it's always heartbreaking." She pauses to crunch a chip. "A few months ago we started hearing stories of zebra sightings in the woods."

"He's a zorse, not a zebra," Leo points out with a wag of his finger.

"No one could get close enough to know what he was," Becca says. "A hiker took a photo of him grazing with wild deer but the photo wasn't very clear. Still, you could tell he was injured—ugly gashes and dried blood all over."

"Oh, that's terrible." Frowning, I set down my cherry juice pouch.

"Terribly terrible." Becca sighs. "When Mom saw the photo, she checked with zoos in the area, but none were missing a zebra. Mom studied the photo and guessed he was a crossbreed. She also guessed he was someone's pet because he was wearing a fly mask. Still, she couldn't find any missing pet reports for a zebroid."

"Zee-what?" I knit my brows.

"I can answer this," Leo says with a knowing lift of his chin. "A zebroid is the offspring of a zebra or other equine, such as a donkey or mule—more commonly known as zedonk, zonkey, zorse, or zebrule."

"Exactly." Becca smiles at him. "Mom went into rescue mode, coming up with a plan to catch Zed. She formed a team of volunteers and they set up a camouflaged corral, not much bigger than this." She gestures around the clean shack. "They placed a bucket of oats to lure Zed inside the corral then propped open the gate. Mom and her team hid close by, waiting."

"Like spies on a stakeout," I say. One of my biggest dreams is to be part of a for-real stakeout.

Becca nods. "They waited for hours and almost quit—then Zed appeared. He sniffed the air like he was suspicious but was too hungry to resist yummy oats. Once Zed entered the corral, the team trapped him inside, quick as a leap. They thought he'd be wild because zorses have personalities more like zebras than tame horses. But then he walked right up to Mom and nuzzled her, tame as a kitten." Becca kisses her purring black kitten. "Zed was in bad shape, though, thin and scarred like he'd been beaten, so it took weeks to get him healthy."

"He looked healthy enough galloping through traffic," I say.

"Traffic?" Leo tilts his head.

"Zed freaked out and ran into traffic this morning," Becca explains, "but Kelsey rushed to the rescue. Like a real hero."

"Hero?" Leo glances at me doubtfully. "Her?"

"Kelsey captured Zed by bribing him with cookies—which was brilliant!" Becca shines her smile on me, and it feels great. "I was afraid Zed would cause an accident or get run over. He's such a sweetie I wish I could keep him—but then I always feel that way about the animals we foster. Well, except for the alligator."

"You have an alligator?" Leo perks up. "Cool!"

"Not so cool when he tries to chomp off your hand." Red, blue, and purple rings glitter as Becca wiggles her fingers. "Luckily I have quick reflexes."

I nod but my thoughts are still on Zed and his mysterious past. "What will happen to Zed now?" I ask.

"We'll foster him until his owners show up."

I frown. "But what if his owners are the ones who hurt him?"

"Without proof of abuse, they'll get him back." Becca crumples the chip bag, tosses it at the trash, but misses, and it bounces onto the floor.

"That's just wrong," I say, picking up the crumpled bag and tossing it into the trash. "He belongs with someone who loves him."

"He'll stay with us until someone claims him— and that could be weeks, months, or longer. No one has responded to the flyers we posted."

"Is that one of the flyers?" Leo asks, pointing to a rolled-up piece of paper poking out from Becca's jeans pocket.

"No, this one is about a lost dog. Officer Skeet, the animal control officer, had a flyer for a missing labradoodle when he stopped by the vet while I was there."

Becca unfolds the paper for us to read.

MISSING LABRADOODLE
Last seen on March 14
near Pleasant and Trent.
Jasper is male, caramel-colored,
three years old, wearing a blue collar.
If found, call 555-2929.
REWARD: $100.

"Poor Jasper," I say. My heart aches for my own dog. At least I can see Handsome when I visit Gran. Jasper's owner may never see him again.

"Officer Skeet asked me to tell all my friends to look for him," Becca adds.

"I will," I say then jump with a jolt as the name "Skeet" clicks in my head. "Wait a minute. Is Officer Skeet related to Burton Skeet?"

"Um...yeah." Becca doesn't meet my gaze, tracing her finger across a stain on the table. "He's Skeet's uncle."

Leo smashes his juice pouch in his hands. "Is he a jerk like Skeet?"

"No—he's super nice and helps lots of animals," Becca adds. "He likes to entertain kids at the hospital by dressing up in fun costumes. Last week he climbed into a well to rescue some baby ducks. Besides, Burt—I mean—Skeet is okay, I mean, he's not bad if you get to know him." Becca glances down so that her hair falls forward and her pink streak brushes her cheek. Is she blushing? Does that mean she actually *likes* Skeet? Yuck.

I say nothing because nothing is the nicest thing I can say about Skeet.

Leo goes silent too, staring out the window. Is he remembering the time Skeet crammed him in a locker and bounced a basketball off the locker door? Or when Skeet tossed Leo's gym clothes into the girls' bathroom?

The clubhouse that is supposed to unite us suddenly seems cramped. The only sounds are the kittens clawing each other playfully in their fuzzy kitty bed and Becca drumming her fingers on the table.

Abruptly, Leo stands and brushes dirt off his vest. "I have an important announcement."

Uh-oh, I think. There's no guessing what Leo will say.

Becca looks uneasy too. "About what?" she asks.

"A serious matter." Leo lifts his shoulders as if carrying a heavy weight of responsibility. "Our club name."

"Great!" Becca smiles. "What?"

"Autonomous Warriors for Felis Catus Silvestris."

Becca's smile fades. "Huh?"

"It's a fitting name for a secret club to protect kittens. Bonus feature—we can each choose a secret robotic name. Mine is Lifelike Electronic Organism Programmed for Observation and Logical Destruction. Get it? It's an acronym for me—L-E-O-P-O-L-D?"

I fold my arms over my chest. "We are *not* robotic warriors."

"Kelsey's right. It's nice of you to come up with a club name but—" Becca pauses, biting her lip. "Sorry, but it's…um…too complicated."

Leo slumps in his chair. "You don't like it?"

"I don't even know what it means," Becca admits.

"But your cousin is a vet tech and your mother rescues animals," he points out. "Surely you recognize the scientific name for cat?"

"Why not just say cat?" Becca's tone is gentle like she's trying really hard not to hurt Leo's feelings. "A club for helping animals needs a short name that represents each of us."

"A valid point." Leo taps his chin thoughtfully. "In that case, I propose we combine words to define ourselves. Each of us will choose one word."

"Oh, I like that. And so does Chris—that's what I'm calling my kitten. It's after the famous designer Christian Dior, who started a movement in the '50s for leopard-print fabrics," Becca adds, smoothing her hand across her yellow-and-black spotted shirt. "We wouldn't be in this clubhouse if not for our kittens. So my word is 'cat.'"

"Curious," Leo says.

"What's curious?" I ask.

"It's my word. Curiosity is the spark that inspires questions, and questions lead to discoveries, and discoveries can change the world."

"Perfect." Becca smiles. "So we have Curious Cat...and what else?"

Becca and Leo turn to me. But I have no clue what to say. I like cats—only Becca already took that word. Curious would have worked too. What else is there? I'm just an ordinary girl with ordinary interests like board games, bike riding, animals, reading, and puzzles. The only thing unusual about me is the backpack hidden on the top shelf of my closet. I created it after reading *Harriet the Spy*.

"Spy," I say before I lose my courage. "That's my word."

They don't laugh or tell me I'm silly. I let out the breath I've been holding.

"It's unanimous." Leo dramatically taps a drumroll on the table with his fingers. "Our club name is Curious Cat Spy Club."

"CCSC for short," Becca adds.

I nod, solemnly gazing down at our kittens. They would have died if Becca, Leo, and I hadn't worked together. We're so different. Becca is outgoing, I'm quiet. And Leo...well, Leo is a challenge. Kids at school would never expect us to be friends but here in our clubhouse we're united. And it's a great feeling.

Leo says we need to make a cat care schedule. Becca volunteers for morning and night shifts since she lives closest. I'll bike over after school (if I'm not grounded for losing Dad's cookies). Leo says he can come after school except on Tuesdays and Thursdays when he has flute and fencing lessons.

We also agree to keep the kittens a secret—which means keeping our friendship a secret too.

Becca comes up with a secret hand-bump: we bump knuckles twice with our fingers curved like a C then trace an S in the air.

"I'll create a secret code and language," Leo offers.

"And I'm the clue holder." I wave the Dalton's Pet Supply receipt from the plastic bag. "This clue may lead us to the villain who dumped our kittens in the trash. We have to check this out soon."

"Tomorrow works for me," Becca says.

Leo nods. "Me too—after we feed the kittens."

We hand-bump on it.

We have a club name, a clubhouse, a clue, and our first mission—track down the cat dumper.

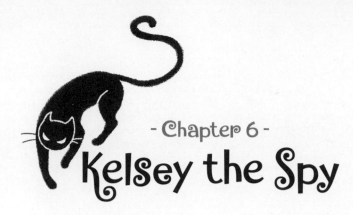

- Chapter 6 -
Kelsey the Spy

"Where were you?" Mom asks when I get home, her gaze sweeping over the dried mud and bird poop on my ripped jeans.

"With new friends," I say, hoping she'll be so glad I'm finally making friends that she won't ask how I got so dirty.

"School friends?" Mom puts down her gardening magazine. She's still wearing her daisy-print smock from the florist shop where she works. "Or friends you met at the library?"

Library? Oh yeah. I forgot I told her I would go to the library after I delivered Dad's cookies… the ones I never delivered. I am so going to be in trouble.

"School friends," I say and move toward the hall, eager to escape to my room. "I better go clean up before dinner."

I make it halfway down the hall before I hear Dad call my name.

"Wait a sec, Kels," he says, coming out of the kitchen with his hands padded in potholders. He smells of spices and tomatoes so I know he's making his special lasagna. He loves cooking and baking so much. I really, really dread telling him what happened to his cookies.

But waiting will only make things worse.

So I swallow the lump in my throat and tell him what happened.

I'm hoping he'll see the humor in a zorse eating his cookies. Before he lost his job, he used to make up jokes and silly puns, and I loved laughing with him. But now he frowns and says, "I thought I could count on you." The disappointment on his face hurts me worse than if he'd yelled.

"I'm sorry, Dad...really..."

He just shakes his head and walks away.

Mom, on the other hand, has plenty to say. "How could you be so irresponsible? Your father does so much for you but when he asks this one thing, you disappoint him. And instead of admitting you lost or broke the cookies you make up a crazy story about a weird animal no one's ever heard of."

"But I'm telling the—" I start to argue just as the phone rings.

Mom points to me and says, "Stand right there, young lady, and don't move a muscle," which is hard to do because the muscles in my face ache from trying not to cry.

When Mom returns minutes later, she's changed. She's still wearing the same comfy Mom jeans and blue-striped blouse. But it's like my real mom has been replaced with a clone who looks exactly like her—except Mom.2 is smiling at me like I'm the best daughter ever. She even hugs me.

"I'm so sorry, Kelsey," she says.

"Huh?"

"That was Mrs. Morales from the Wild Oaks Animal Sanctuary on the phone. She called to say how grateful she is that you saved her zorse. Why didn't you tell us you were a hero?"

"I...I didn't think I was," I say, confused.

"Oh, honey, I'm sorry I didn't believe your story," she says.

"You mean...you aren't mad about the cookies?"

"Of course not!" She hugs me again. "I'm proud of you, and your dad will be too when I explain how you saved a rare animal from being run over."

She goes to find Dad while I sink onto the couch, trying to sort out what just happened. Becca got her mom to call my mom? Wow! Thank you, Becca!

Instead of being grounded or scrubbing toilets, after dinner Dad rewards me with a huge home-made caramel-chip cookie with the word *hero* in purple icing.

My brother and twin sisters, who usually ignore me because they're older and super busy, beg me to share. So I end up with only a small bite of my hero cookie. But it's delicious.

Later when I'm alone in my bedroom, the apartment is quiet except for the murmur from the TV in my parents' room. My room is so small only a twin bed, a desk, and a narrow dresser fit in it. But I love my room and it's better than sharing with my sisters (double doses of bossy, messy, and noisy).

I tiptoe over to the closet and climb on a stool to reach the highest shelf. I feel around until my fingertips touch cloth. I pull down the green back-pack. Not an ordinary backpack—my spy pack.

After reading *Harriet the Spy*, I decided to become a spy when I grow up. But then I figured, why wait till I grow up? I can eavesdrop now to uncover all kinds of secrets. When I spy on someone, I try to guess their secret thoughts— because all thoughts *are* secret. Even if someone tells you what they're thinking, you can never be sure it's the truth. But if you watch, listen, and lip-read, you can find out interesting stuff. Like everyone thinks my algebra teacher Mr. Armstrong hates kids because he never smiles. But once, when he thought we were all busy with a quiz, I saw him mouth "Miss you" to a framed photo on his desk of two dark-haired kids—a boy and a girl—about my age. When I looked him up online, I found out his ex-wife recently moved their kids to Canada. All the other students think he's mean, but I think he's just sad because he misses his kids.

Secrets are collectible, like game cards or favorite books, and when I discover someone's secret it becomes my secret too. I never gossip or hurt anyone with what I find out. I just want to know the truth, like detectives in mystery novels compelled to solve crimes. As the youngest in a busy, talented family, collecting secrets makes me feel less average and more interesting.

My spy pack is a work in progress. Last week I added a small mirror after reading a mystery where the sleuth used a mirror to collect a fingerprint.

Other items in my pack are:

Black knit cap

Plastic gloves

Magnifying glass

Laser pointer

Graphite powder and brush

Lock picks

Wire and wire cutters

Mini-cam

Recording pen

Flashlight

Rain jacket

Baggies

Notepad

Energy bars

Sadly, my spy pack doesn't get much use. Spying on my siblings is boring. All my sisters talk about is guys and my brother is too busy applying for college scholarships. Not many spy ops for a kid— but that's going to change now thanks to the CCSC.

I pull the Dalton's receipt from my pocket and carefully zip it into a baggie.

My first piece of crime evidence ever!

Should I sprinkle it with graphite powder to check for fingerprints? That would be fun but it would also mess up the receipt. And even if I found prints other than my own it's not like I have a fingerprint database for comparison like a crime lab. I'll learn more from talking to the clerk who matches the employee ID number on the receipt. Other info on the receipt is helpful too: items purchased (cat, dog, and fish food) with date, time, and prices.

A lot of clues to follow, I think as I yawn.

I tuck the baggie with the receipt inside my spy pack, return the pack to my closet, and, finally, after the most exciting day of my life, I fall asleep.

- Chapter 7 -
Secret Friends

I'm reaching into my locker for my English book Monday morning when I hear Becca's voice. Spinning around, I start to call her name then clamp my mouth shut. Oops! Almost forgot we're keeping the kittens and our club a secret. If other kids saw us together they'd get curious and ask questions. Like Leo said, curiosity leads to discoveries—and we don't want our secrets discovered.

Still, a secret friendship feels lonely.

I sneak a glance as Becca heads my way, arm in arm with the Sparklers. That's what her group of four call themselves for obvious glittery reasons. For obvious *spy* reasons, I am not a fan of glitter. Although I think Becca's glittery hair looks really cute curling above the tiger design on her denim jacket.

She walks by so close I could reach out and touch her. Yet I say nothing. She doesn't say anything either. But after she passes, she glances over her shoulder and winks at me. I wink back.

It's not until lunch that I see Leo—sitting solo in his usual corner and eating from a bag lunch while he types on his tablet. Leo can be annoying, but he's never boring, and I'm curious to see what he's writing. What sort of robot is he designing? Would he show me if I asked? If we ate lunch together we could talk about the kittens and I'd offer him one of Dad's yummy cream cakes.

But I plop down at my usual table with Ann Marie Sanchez and Tori Eye. Raven-haired Ann Marie is petite and has the whitest teeth I've ever seen (her mom is my dentist). Tori has long caramel-brown hair and is tall enough to be a model but she'd rather shoot basketballs. Before I moved away, we were neighbors and we still sit together for lunch at school. They're both sporty girls with busy track-basketball-soccer schedules. They love to gossip and I love to listen, so hanging out with them is a win-win even for a nonathletic type like me.

But I can't concentrate today. I chew my apple slowly, nodding often so they think I'm listening while my gaze drifts over to Leo. I catch him looking at me a few times too. And we both sneak peeks at Becca.

Longest. Lunch. Ever.

During my afternoon classes I fidget, doodle cats instead of taking notes, and stare longingly out the window. How are the kittens doing? Were they cold last night? Did they spill their water bowl or run out of cat food? Are they scared? Are they safe?

When the final bell rings, I bolt from my chair so quickly I almost forget to grab my backpack. I grab the straps and slip them over my shoulders. Then I rush past my locker without stopping toward my bike. Usually I walk the few blocks to and from school, but for CCSC reasons, from now on I'm biking.

I'm the first to arrive at our clubhouse, and when I step inside I panic.

The kitten bed is empty!

I call "Kitty, kitty" and hear mews and follow the sound to three kittens curled together beneath the broken grandfather clock. The kittens spring up, mewing as they scamper over to me.

I scoop them in my arms, trying not to play favorites. (Though of course Honey is *my* fur-baby.) I cuddle, kiss, and murmur sweet words. Their food dish is empty. I gently place the kittens on the floor, and I pop open a can of cat food. The kittens frisk and wiggle around my shoes like they're dancing a happy-kitty dance. While they chow down, I refill their water dish and scoop clean the litter box.

The kittens are licking the can clean when I hear a strange humming sound.

Curious (and a little scared), I peek through the window just as Leo glides to a stop on the strangest skateboard I've ever seen. It's electric with super-sized wheels and lots of metal and wiring. Leo clicks a handheld remote which shuts off the motor.

"Where'd you get that?" I point as he flips up the skateboard and props it near the shack door.

"It's a Leo Polanski original," Leo says proudly. "I designed and built it myself. The gyroscope and accelerometer sensors keep it balanced and the all-terrain tires steer by a rocker switch."

I have no clue what he's talking about. "Cool skateboard," I say.

"Gyro-board," he corrects.

I shrug. "Looks like fancy skateboard."

"Fancy?" He spits the word like it's an insult. "I'll have you know, this highly improved gyroboard is far superior to an ordinary skateboard."

I roll my eyes and wish there was an improved version of Leo—one that came without sound.

Half an hour later, Leo is tinkering with the grandfather clock and I'm dangling a string for the kittens when Becca finally arrives.

"What took you so long?" I ask her.

She sets down a paper bag and sighs. "I had trouble getting away from Mom. She kept finding chores for me to do and when I tried to sneak cat food, she caught me so I made up a story about donating cans for a school food drive. She thought it was weird that I wanted food for pets and not people but she let me take two cans. If I take any more, she'll get suspicious."

"But we'll need more—and soon." Frowning, I sink down on a blue-flowered chair with a wobbly leg. "I only have six dollars left over from birthday money. I don't get an allowance and I'm too young for a job."

Becca frowns. "Mom pays me to help with the animals but I used it all and borrowed more...so now I owe her money."

"What'd you buy?" I ask.

"Um...shoes." Becca blushes. "Snow leopard print canvas shoes."

"Ooh, sounds cute. Totally worth it," I say, which wins me one of her brightest smiles.

I expect Leo to make a snarky comment but he's staring out the window, mumbling to himself. After a moment, he turns back to us. "With the $8.70 I have, plus Kelsey's six dollars, we can buy $14.70 of cat supplies. According to my calculations, estimating the cost of cat food and litter, that will last us five days."

"And then what?" I pick up Honey and hold her close to my heart. "We need to make some money."

"But how?" Becca flips a curl from her face, worry lines around her dark eyes.

We all look at each other as if hoping someone else has a great idea. But no one says anything.

I stare down at an ink stain on the table like it's sucking me into a hopeless black hole. I hate not having money. My parents hate it too. They don't think I hear when they talk about money troubles but at night their voices come through my bedroom walls loud and clear. Dad is getting really depressed waiting for a callback from one of his job interviews. And Mom cries sometimes when they talk about our old house. Money—or lack of it anyway—ruins everything. I need a miracle to find lots of money...fast!

We were so lucky to find the kittens, I think. If Zed hadn't run through traffic, if I hadn't bribed him with Dad's cookies, if Becca hadn't taken me through the alley to avoid Skeet, if I hadn't heard sounds in the dumpster, and if Becca hadn't asked Leo to help us—the kittens would have died. So many things that seemed wrong at the time happened in exactly the right way. But one wrong thing is still very wrong.

"We have five days to earn some money. But I want to find the cat dumper right now." I whip out the Dalton's Pet Supply receipt from my pocket. "Who wants to go with me?"

- Chapter 8 -
A Fishy Clue

Dalton's Pet Supply is only a few miles away. Becca and I ride our bikes while Leo, the show-off, zip-zaps ahead on his gyro-board.

When we reach the store, Becca and I lock up our bikes. Leo flips up his bike and keys in a code to set an electric lock that will shriek a warning if anyone tries to steal his gyro-board. I'm a little impressed, but I don't tell him.

As I start for the store Leo blocks me with his arm. "Kelsey, give me the receipt. I'll do the questioning."

"But I found the clue." I purse my lips stubbornly.

"I've prepared a list of questions." He waves two pages printed from his computer. "According to my calculations, these are the most logical questions to ask the clerk."

I skim the pages. "Twenty-seven questions! You can't be serious."

"I am *always* serious."

"I've noticed."

"Thanks," he says like this is a compliment, not a complaint. "I won't ask all the questions. No more than twenty-two. I tossed in the last few for kicks and snickers." He actually snickers. "I don't really need to know the clerk's IQ or his favorite poem."

"Forget your list," I tell him. "I'll do the talking."

"But you'll mess up."

"Will not!"

"Fine," he says with an eye roll. "At least study my list so you don't say anything stupid."

I start to tell him what he can do with his list but Becca steps between us like a referee at a wrestling match. "Enough! Stop arguing and talk to the clerk together. I'll be in the cat care aisle pretending I don't know either of you." She flips her dark curls over her shoulders and stomps into the store.

"Do you think she's mad?" Leo asks, frowning.

"Nah." I shake my head. "Just having a drama moment."

"Is that something girls do a lot?" Leo looks genuinely confused.

"Not just girls. Boys too," I say with a pointed look at him. But as usual he doesn't get my sarcasm.

"Well...good. I guess," Leo says. He actually smiles and lets me enter the store first.

With the receipt in my hand, I walk up to the check-out counter.

A plump, black-eyed girl with shiny pink braces stands behind the counter. She's wearing a name badge but I already know her name is Felicity because she hangs out with my sisters. Like most of my sisters' friends, she ignores me because she's in high school and I'm a lowly mid-grader. But I'm always listening and have collected a few of her secrets.

"Can I help you?" Felicity flashes a fake smile. I can tell she doesn't remember me.

I show her the receipt. "I'm trying to find out who this belongs to."

"Isn't it yours?" Felicity glances down at the paper.

"No," I answer honestly.

"But you have it?" She taps a green pen impatiently on the counter, her drawn-on brows arching with suspicion.

"We found it." I consider telling her about the kittens until I remember she has a pet bird and doesn't like cats. What can I say to convince her to help us?

I'm still thinking about this when Leo pushes me aside. "My father always saves his receipts for business reasons," Leo says.

"Good for him," Felicity replies in a totally bored tone.

"Well, yes." Leo nods. "Whoever lost this receipt may need it for business records. Tell me who lost it, and I'll return it."

Felicity narrows her eyes at Leo. "Why do you care about someone you don't even know?"

"I believe in paying forward acts of kindness. Someday I might lose something and I'll expect it to be returned."

Leo sounds so sincere I almost believe him. But Felicity isn't buying it. I've heard her gripe about her "lying, cheating" ex-boyfriend so I know she doesn't trust guys. Leo should have let me talk.

"Can't help you," Felicity snaps. "We don't have a database that matches customers to receipts."

I point to the receipt. "That's an employee number, right? Could we talk to the clerk who made this sale?"

She flicks her gaze down at the receipt and laughs. "That's *my* number. Unless you're buying something, we're done." She motions for the next customer in line.

That went well—*not*.

"I didn't get to ask any of my questions," Leo gripes as we turn away from the counter.

"Let's just get out of here," I say, discouraged.

"Where did Becca go?" Leo asks, craning his neck to look around the aisles.

I stand on my tiptoes to see over counters and spot Becca's dark ponytail in an aisle labeled *Fish*. She's not alone. She's smiling at a lanky guy with brown hair wearing a red Dalton's Pet Supply shirt. When she sees us, she waves us over.

"Meet Pete," she says, gesturing to the guy who's probably in college and cute in a geeky way. "He's interested in exotic animals so I was telling him about Wild Oaks Animal Sanctuary. And he might be able to help with our fish problem."

"Fish problem?" I say.

"You know." Becca gives me a *look*. "How Wild Oaks has an alligator pond but no pond for the koi fish we rescue. Show him the receipt."

Since when do fish need rescuing? I wonder,

feeling like I'm reading a mystery that's missing a chapter. Still, I hand over the receipt.

"Sorry, I wasn't working when this sale was made." Pete shakes his hair that's so shaggy he reminds me of a sheep dog. "And I can't keep track of all the customers who buy fish food."

I sigh. My clue is leading nowhere fast.

"But I do know something that could help." Pete moves down the aisle of fish food to tap a bag with colorful pictures of spotted fish. "We stock this brand of koi fish food at the request of a few customers."

"Can you give us names?" Becca asks eagerly.

"Never been good with names. Besides, my boss wouldn't like me talking about our customers. Still, that doesn't mean we can't discuss geography." He leans closer to us and whispers, "There's this street where all the fancy-schmancy custom-built homes came with fish ponds. The koi owners I know live there."

"Where?" Leo, Becca, and I ask in unison.

"Willow Rose Lane."

We thank Pete and hurry out the store. When we reach the bike rack Becca explains, "While I was waiting for you, I saw Pete stocking fish food and remembered koi fish food was on the receipt. Lots of people have cats and dogs, but not many keep both cats and koi."

"Good thinking," I say. A breeze whips up, tangling my hair as I bend down to unlock my bike chain. Pushing back my hair, I ask, "How expensive are koi?"

"Butterfly koi can cost over a thousand dollars." Becca grabs the handlebars of her bike and kicks up the stand. "Since I couldn't tell Pete about our kittens, I said I hoped to find a foster home for abandoned koi fish."

Leo tilts his head curiously. "Who abandons koi fish?"

"No one—but Pete doesn't know that." Becca grins. "And he gave us a good lead on where to look for the cat dumper."

"Willow Rose Lane," I say with growing excitement because I know what this means.

I'm going on a stakeout.

- Chapter 9 -
Mis-Stake-Out

There are eighteen houses on Willow Rose Lane, and they all look alike. Spanish adobe style with stone paths winding up to double front doors, perfectly mowed lawns, three-car garages, stained-glass windows, and wrought-iron gates guarding backyards.

Becca and I bike around the block with Leo skate-boarding beside us like we're just out for a ride. We meet on the sidewalk on the corner beneath a shady willow tree to strategize.

The sun is sinking behind treetops and a breeze shivers through branches creating shadows on the road that seem alive. Hidden from view in the shadows, I feel like a for-real spy instead of an ordinary school girl. I imagine I'm James Bond's daughter, Jamie, or maybe something more exotic like Jasmine. Yeah, I like that—Jazzy Bond, girl sleuth.

Leo glides up on his gyro-board with the balance of a gymnast as he checks his cell phone. "I'm scrolling through this cool real estate app for information on this street." In his button-down shirt, black slacks, and polished loafers he looks more like a businessman than a kid. "We need to determine which homes have koi fish."

"Or look for a sad mother cat without kittens," Becca says.

"And anyone acting suspicious," I add.

Leo glances at his phone and he nods. "I've circled this block fourteen times but the fences around the backyards are too high to tell which houses have fish ponds. Riding around in circles gets us nowhere. We need a strategy."

"We could go door-to-door selling something like when I sold Girl Scout cookies," Becca suggests.

Leo scowls. "Do I look like a Girl Scout?"

"You can wear a wig," I tease.

"I'll loan you my old Girl Scout outfit," Becca adds.

"Not funny." Leo glares at us when we burst out laughing.

We stop laughing abruptly when there's shouting from a yard two houses down. A thirtyish woman wearing a purple robe and fuzzy slippers waves a net in the air, stringy brown hair whipping around her face like an evil witch in a fairy tale.

"Get out of here!" the woman yells.

Is she yelling at us? I grab my handlebars, ready to hop on my bike and zoom out of here fast. But she isn't looking our way. She's waving the fishing net at something behind a crimson bush.

"I warned you to stay away or I'd kill you!" She lifts the net high like she's wielding a deadly ax.

I've never heard of death by net. And since when does a killer wear fuzzy slippers? Still, you can't tell what people are capable of by looking at them.

I hear a hiss as Witchy Woman lunges with her net and a smoke-gray cat leaps to the top of a nearby fence. I glimpse a shiny pink collar around the cat's neck before it scampers down the fence.

The woman may be wearing fuzzy slippers but she moves fast as she chases after the cat, waving the net.

"Get back here!" she shouts, running around the bushes.

The fence stops where it meets the house, and the cat can't go any farther. The cat looks around as if searching for an escape route. Before it can spring to safety, the woman lunges with the net and scoops up the cat.

"Got you!" she shouts in triumph. With a laugh, she carries the net with the cat struggling and screeching in terror toward the front door.

"I have to help that cat!" Becca starts to run toward the house.

"Wait!" I grab the corner of her zebra-striped scarf and yank her back. "You can't just go rushing into a stranger's yard."

Leo nods. "What if the cat belongs to her? We can't stop her from bringing her own cat inside the house."

"No one threatens to kill her own cat," Becca argues. "Listen to it cry—the poor thing is terrified."

"It's not her cat," I say, adding up the clues. "She yelled at it to get out of her yard. But when it didn't, she tried to catch it. And it's not a stray because it's wearing a collar. So I suspect it's a neighbor's cat."

"Cats love to explore," Becca says, nodding. "Unfortunately the cat picked the house of a cat-hater."

"You don't think she'll really kill it?" Leo asks, running his fingers nervously through his blond hair.

"I've heard of people doing worse," Becca adds with a shudder.

We huddle together, watching as the woman reaches her porch. She smiles while the cat thrashes, its claws tangled in netting, snagged like a fly in a spider web.

"Maybe we can't stop her, but I know someone who can." Becca whips out her phone. "I'll call Officer Skeet—he'll know what to do."

"Good idea. Hurry!" I urge.

Leo frowns, probably because the animal control officer is also the uncle of his enemy. But I only care about saving the cat.

I clench my hands and hold my breath as the witchy woman walks up her porch steps. She can't open the door while holding the net, so she shifts the net to one hand and balances it on a brick planter. As she grasps the doorknob, the cat untangles its feet and springs out. It sails over the porch and lands gracefully on the lawn.

"Run, kitty!" Becca whispers, putting down her phone.

"Get back here!" the woman shouts, her net dropping to the steps with a clatter. "You can't get away from me!"

But the cat is already across her yard. It leaps over a hedge and races down the sidewalk faster than a zorse.

I want to applaud but we *are* undercover so I keep my voice low. "Score one for the cat."

"If he's smart, he'll never come back," Becca says.

"The woman's hostility toward the cat is suspicious," Leo adds.

"Highly suspicious," I agree. "And she has a fishing net that she might use for koi fish."

"She's too mean to have pets." Becca tightens her hands into fists like Warrior Becca, Defender of Helpless Creatures. "I can't stand people who abuse animals."

"Me either," I agree. "Anyone that cruel to a cat probably hates kittens too. She's my top suspect for cat-dumper."

"We'll need proof," Leo says.

"I made a cap-cam," I offer. "You can wear like a hat that records everything you see. But that would mean actually going into the yard."

"Too risky," Leo says. "I'll set up a remote surveillance cam."

"You have one?" I ask, surprised. I've seen high-tech cams in my spy catalogs and they're crazy expensive.

"I will by tomorrow with aerial capabilities." Leo pulls out his tablet from his back pocket.

"Huh?" Becca scrunches her forehead. "You mean a flying camera?"

"Much better," he says with a mysterious smile.

"It sounds great...whatever it is." Becca gives Leo a thumps up. "And I'll check my social contacts to see if any of my friends live around her or know someone who docs."

They turn to me, waiting to hear what skills I have to offer. I can lip-read, know surveillance tactics, and have a spy pack. But I hesitate, gnawing on my lower lip. I've never shared these secrets with anyone. *Just say it*, I urge myself. But the words are trapped in my throat. I'm used to watching and listening. I'm not so good at talking about myself.

My club mates look at me, waiting.

"Um...I know a little about..." I move deeper into the shade on the sidewalk. "I mean...well, actually, a lot about spying." I take a huge breath then slowly let it out and tell them everything, starting with *Harriet the Spy*.

"Wow!" Becca says. "Lip-reading is coolness."

"What's in your spy pack?" Leo asks.

"The cap-cam I already told you about, and a flashlight, a laser pen, a magnifying glass, graphite powder, wire, a recording pen, and a lot more."

Becca shifts her bicycle so she's facing me and mouths, "Where did you find the spy stuff?"

"Internet and thrift stores," I answer out loud.

"What?" Leo asks, looking puzzled.

"You really can lip-read?" Becca mouths.

"Yes," I say proudly.

"Whatever you're doing, stop it," Leo orders, hands on his hips, looking suspiciously between us.

"Just girl talk." Becca giggles. "Kelsey is just made of coolness."

I smile like a compliment from Becca isn't a big deal but inside I'm flipping cartwheels. Becca, the nicest and most interesting girl ever, thinks I'm coolness.

"You're both acting weird," Leo complains, hopping onto his gyro-board. "There's nothing I can accomplish today, so I'm leaving."

"Are we meeting at the Skunk Shack tomorrow?"

I move my bike from the shadows, lacy willow leaves rustling overhead.

"My fencing class is from three to four." Leo powers up the robotized board with a click of his remote. "I can't help with the kittens but I can meet you after my lesson.""

"Kelsey and I can take care of the kittens then we meet you here," Becca suggests, hopping on her bike. "What time can you make it, Leo?"

"At 4:34," Leo says with a nod.

"Works for me." I try not to giggle but it's funny how precise Leo is.

"See you then!" Becca pushes off with her foot. She waves as she pedals in the direction of downtown Sun Flower.

Leo and I wheel off toward the suburbs. We only live a few blocks apart. I know which house is his because I pass it on my way to school. His two-story house is milky white. Even the front yard is white — carnation flowers in a pale stone planter and tiny white rocks instead of a green lawn. It makes me think of winter and Christmas snow all year long.

So Leo and I are riding together, sort of. It's awkward because we just happen to be going the same direction, and without Becca, there isn't any conversation. We're in the same club so we're friends...right? I like him when he's not talking down to me like he knows everything. I know a lot too—especially when it comes to secrets.

My bike wheels and Leo's souped-up skate wheels whirl side-by-side for a block until Leo zooms ahead of me on his gyro-board. Feeling competitive, I pedal faster, so now I'm the one in the lead. He speeds up, taking the lead again.

We go back and forth like this—me in the lead then him. It's not like we're in a race. We're both just too stubborn to slow down. My legs pump so hard I can hardly breathe.

We don't slow down—until we see the dog.

- Chapter 10 -
Dog Gone

A medium-sized brown dog with curly fur scampers down the sidewalk. He looks familiar so I coast over for a closer look. He has a collar but no leash or owner running after him. When I get near, he wags his tail so I know he's friendly. He must live around here, I decide. So I ride past him—until a startling thought strikes me.

I slam on my brakes.

Brown dog. Blue collar.

The missing dog from the flyer!

I spin a wheelie and think back to the flyer Becca showed us. I can't remember all the details, only that the missing dog is a labradoodle with a blue collar and his name begins with J.

I nudge down my bike's kickstand and offer my hand to the dog with my palm up so I can pass the sniff test. He wags his tail. I talk to him, trying out the name Jasper, and he wags some more.

"What are you doing?" Leo asks, rolling to a stop beside me.

"Shssh! Keep your voice low or you might scare him. I'm checking out his collar."

"Why?"

"Isn't it obvious, Sherlock? He looks like a labradoodle, he's alone, brown, and wearing a *blue* collar."

"Oh!" Leo clicks off his gyro-board. "The missing dog from Becca's flyer. Do you think it's the same dog?"

"He fits the description and he's wandering by himself." I lean closer to check the collar. "A license and rabies tag—but no phone number."

"I'll call the number from the lost flyer," Leo offers.

"You remember it?" I ask in amazement.

"No. But it'll be online." Leo whips out his cell phone. "*Jasper* plus *missing dog* plus *phone number*...found it!"

As he calls the number, I hope, hope, hope we can reach Jasper's owner. Losing a pet is the worst feeling ever. It still hurts to remember when I had to leave my dog with Gran Nola. Handsome loves Gran's big yard and special homemade doggie treats, but I know he misses me too.

"Three rings so far," Leo reports. "Four and... Good afternoon, I'm calling about your missing dog. My friend and I found...What? Are you sure?" There's a long silence as Leo listens. I try to figure out what's being said on the other line, but Leo isn't giving any clues.

Finally Leo says, "Thanks," then shuts off his phone.

"Well, *what?*" I keep petting the dog so he doesn't run off. "Is he or is he not Jasper?"

"Not." Leo sighs and slips the phone into his pocket. "Jasper was returned by an old lady who found him hiding in her garage. She uses a cane and wasn't strong enough to carry him, but when she opened her car door, he jumped inside. She called the number on the flyer and brought Jasper home."

"I'm so glad Jasper's safe," I say, imagining a reunion with tail wags and hugs.

"The old woman didn't even want the reward," Leo adds, "but Jasper's owner insisted."

"She deserved it." I look down at the friendly brown dog licking my hand. "But if that dog was returned—who does this dog belong to?"

"Me." A girlish voice says from behind us. "I'm Emma."

Turning, I see a pretty olive-skinned girl holding a red leash that dangles to her purple-laced sneakers. She looks about ten but is at least three inches taller than me. Immediately the dog bounds over and jumps on her.

"Down, Roscoe! You are so bad," the girl says as she clips the leash onto Roscoe's collar. Her black ponytails bounce with her as she turns back to us. "He broke free from his leash and I've been chasing him for blocks. I was worried he'd get lost like my friend Haley's dog did."

"He's really friendly," I say. "What breed is he?"

Emma pauses to catch her breath before answering. "Purebred mutt."

Leo shakes his head. "A purebred can't also be a mutt. That's an oxymoron."

"Watch what you call my dog," she snaps. "He's really smart."

"But he can't be a purebred," Leo argues.

"He's a one-of-a-kind pure Roscoe," Emma

insists with a snap of her fingers. "Pure shepherd, lab, husky, and poodle mix."

"She told you," I tease Leo.

But Leo has his "thinking" look. He tilts his head at Emma. "Did you say your neighbor's dog was lost?"

"Not anymore." Emma's ponytails flop as she shakes her head. "Toby was gone for two days until a tattooed guy recognized him from one of the reward flyers. Other pets have gone missing too. I'm so glad Roscoe wasn't lost overnight—that would have been so scary. Thanks for catching him."

"Glad to help." I pat Roscoe's head. "He's a sweetheart."

"Sweet, but hard to slow down when I walk him. Come on, Roscoe," Emma says in a firm voice. "We're going home."

I'm smiling as I watch them walk away. I glance over at Leo, expecting him to look happy too, but he's staring at a crack in the pavement. "What's with the weird expression?" I ask.

"I'm thinking about Toby and Jasper."

"Why? They aren't lost anymore."

"Too many dogs have gone missing."

"It's just a coincidence," I say.

"I don't believe in coincidences."

Then I think of something else that seems odd, and my mind spins. I swing onto my bike, balancing on the toes of my sneakers. I remember Emma saying other dogs had been missing. Could the gray cat who escaped from Witchy Woman be a lost pet too?

How many pets are missing in Sun Flower?

"Now you're the one with a weird look," Leo says as he coasts his gyro-board beside me.

"Not weird—inspired." I grin. "I just had a great idea that will help us care for our kittens."

- Chapter 11 -
Bird-Drone Blast-Off

I can't wait to research my idea online, but when I get home, my brother has custody of the computer—of course. I plead with him to let me use it, but Kyle seems to think applying to colleges is more important. I liked him better before we moved, when he was a slacker, shooting hoops with his buddies instead of obsessed with his future. Fortunately we have a family rule about spending no more than an hour on the computer, so Kyle finally gets off.

It takes only five minutes to strike gold on the Pet Finder site with reports of missing animals. There are over a dozen listings for Sun Flower—lost dogs, cats, rabbits, and even a pig. I print them out and file the papers in a CCSC Pet Project folder.

The next day at school I'm bursting to tell Becca my idea. Leo already knows, and—shocker— he likes it. But it's impossible to talk to Becca privately because she's always with her jabbering group of Sparklers.

I can't wait to see her at the Skunk Shack. Leo has his fencing class, so it'll be just Becca and me, which is nice. I like her so much, and I have this secret hope that she'll get bored with the Sparklers and become my best friend. But I know it'll never happen so I add this secret to my collection.

I'm popping open a can of food for the kittens when Becca steps into the clubhouse. I'm here first because Becca stopped by her house to change from her chic clothes into comfy jeans and a T-shirt. Our after-school routine works great. My parents don't mind if I'm late as long as I'm home in time for dinner. They're just glad I have a friend and have stopped complaining about moving to an apartment.

"Ta-da!" Becca says with a wave of her hands as she enters the shack. "You are looking at the social sleuthing queen. I found out who lives in three houses on Willow Rose Lane."

"I bow down to your royal skills." I toss an empty cat food can into a garbage bag. "Details, please."

"You know who Sophia Ramirez is, right?"

I nod, well aware of her Sparkler friends: Tyla, Sophia, and Chloe.

"Sophia's grandmother lives at 343 Willow Rose. Only Nana Ramirez doesn't have a dog or fish. She breeds Persian cats and is super sweet to her kitties, so cross her off your suspect list. But her neighbor, Mrs. Tupin, is way suspicious," Becca adds, her dark eyes shining. "Mrs. Tupin is vice president of the Sun Flower Garden Club and obsessed with her prize-winning roses. And her address is 347, plus she has koi fish."

We've ridden around the block so many times I have the addresses memorized. "Witchy Woman!" I exclaim, thinking of the woman in the robe and slippers who threatened to kill the gray cat.

"She did look like a wicked witch when she caught that poor cat in her net," Becca says, punching open a juice packet from a cooler and handing one to me too. "I bet she's the one who dumped our kittens. And she probably did in their mother too."

"You think?" I say, leaning closer.

Becca nods. "I have a theory that the mother cat, probably a stray, had her kittens in Mrs. Tupin's yard. Mama Cat either ran off or something bad happened to her. Then the witch found the kittens and dumped them in the trash."

"Or the mother cat belongs to Witchy Woman," I suggest, remembering that the receipt we found included cat food. "But your scenario still works— she didn't want any kittens so she dumped them."

"Our poor kitties." Becca shudders. "I'm so glad we found them."

"Me too. That horrible witch should be punished."

"She will be if we can prove she's guilty," Becca says.

"We still have to investigate other clues. You said you know who lives in a third house on Willow Rose?"

"Yeah, he lives in the last house on the street— but he's not a suspect," Becca says quickly.

"We have to investigate all clues. What did Sophia tell you?"

"Um...it wasn't Sophia...it was someone else." Becca turns away from me to watch the kittens frisk in and out of a box. "It's his uncle who lives on Willow Rose Lane—and has a fish pond too. But his uncle is the nicest man ever and would never, *ever* hurt an animal."

Something clicks in my head and I gasp. "Burton Skeet's uncle!"

"Well...yeah." She drums her fingers nervously on the table.

"You talked to Skeet!" I stand up to face her. "But you were avoiding him a few days ago and told me you didn't want to talk about him."

"I don't want to."

"But you talked *to* him," I accuse. "Why?"

She shrugs, her cheeks reddening.

"You can't possibly like him?"

"Not that way," she says sharply. "And I don't want to talk about it."

Abruptly, she turns away from me and over to the kittens, watching them play. I wait for Becca to explain why she's being so weird about Skeet. But I don't want to make her mad. So I join her on the floor, playing with the kittens. After a while, we're talking again like the awkwardness never happened.

"So where's your famous spy pack?" Becca asks.

"Famous? Not even." I shrug. "It's at home since it's too heavy to lug around school with my textbooks. But I did bring this." I hand her my CCSC Pet Project folder.

"What project?" she asks.

"Earning money for our club." I cross my fingers and hope she approves.

"Lost pet reports?" Becca pushes back her dark hair as she flips through the papers. "Oh, here's a listing for Jasper. But he's already been found."

"There's one for Toby too," I say. "I even found one for a missing gray cat, which sounds like the one that escaped Witchy Woman. Too bad we didn't know she was missing."

"Lots of pets are still missing," Becca says.

"When we go back to Willow Rose Lane, we'll look for the gray cat and other missing animals. We'll return them and if we're offered any rewards we'll use the money for cat supplies. Finding lost pets is a perfect CCSC project."

"But doing it for a reward feels wrong," Becca says, frowning.

"We won't ask for money—we'll just look for lost pets while we ride our bikes. Not all pet owners offer rewards, and that's okay. I'm happy to help for nothing. But if grateful owners give us a reward, it would be rude to refuse. Besides we don't want the

money for ourselves. It's all for helping animals."
Honey frisks up my jeans and purrs in my lap.
"Like our kittens."

"It's not that easy to find lost pets," Becca
points out.

"We already found one missing dog."

"Roscoe wasn't actually missing," Becca says.
"And Jasper had already been returned."

"Returned for one hundred dollars! We could
have had that reward if we'd found him first." I
point to the print-outs. "Twenty-five dollars for
the gray cat, one hundred for a Chihuahua, and
seventy-five for a potbellied pig."

"We only need enough money to feed the kittens
till the Humane Society fund-raiser next month,"
Becca says.

"We'll donate extra money to the fund-raiser,"
I suggest.

"Great idea!" Becca grins. "And after the fund-
raiser, Wild Oaks will have room for the kittens. I
may even talk Mom into letting me keep them."

"I wish Honey could live with me." I sigh. My
dog is with Gran and my cat will be with Becca.
Will I ever be able to keep my own pet?

"I'll take good care of Honey and you can visit

her whenever you want."

"Thanks," I say, sharing a sympathetic look with Becca. I like her more each time we hang out.

"Look at my silly kitten biting his own tail," Becca says, giggling. "Chris is kind of klutzy. And I love him so much."

I whisper, "Love you, Honey" as I hold my kitten against my heart.

Once we're done with the kittens, we slip into spy mode. We ride our bikes to rendezvous with Leo beneath the willow tree on a shady corner of Willow Rose Lane.

"Leo, good news," I say as we join him.

"What?" He glances up from a small metal gadget with pointed angles and lots of wires he's tinkering with.

"Becca likes the lost pet idea," I tell him.

"Uh-huh," Leo says in a distracted voice, adjusting gears with a tiny screwdriver. He's working on a tiny robot that looks just like a sparrow with wings on hinges and reflective eyes like camera lenses.

"Kelsey printed out a list of the pets to look out for," Becca tells Leo, her silver Sparkler necklace swaying as she bends over to study his metal bird.

"Be on the lookout for a the gray cat we saw last time, a brown Chihuahua, and a pig," I say.

"Pig?" Leo looks up from his tinkering.

"Potbellied." Becca taps the print-out showing a stout brown pig the size of a basset hound. "We fostered one once and he was really smart. But he was huge because his owners overfed him. They don't need much food but people think they're like garbage disposals and feed them then decide they don't want a chubby pig."

"But it's not the pig's fault," Leo argues.

"Tell that to the owners." Becca throws up her hands, her dark eyes blazing. "Do *not* get me started about irresponsible pet owners. When I give tours at Wild Oaks Animal Sanctuary, I lecture people about proper pet care. Mom says I'm too bossy, but I'm just trying to help."

"I'd love a tour of your sanctuary," I say. "It sounds like you have so many cool animals. Do you really sleep with a snoring goat?"

"Every night," she says, chuckling. "Sinbad is a baby pygmy goat and thinks I'm his mom. He's scared of thunderstorms so he started sleeping in my room—which is okay except for the snoring."

"Is he potty trained?" I ask.

"I wish! But he wears a diaper."

"A goat in a diaper?" I laugh. "I'd like to see that."

"So come over for a tour tomorrow," she says with that friendly smile I like so much.

"Me too?" Leo sets down a wrench and looks up at Becca hopefully. "I really want to see the alligator."

"Sure. And you can meet Mom too. She doesn't know about our club but I told her I have two new friends."

Friends. I smile to myself. Not best friends, but it's a good start.

"Prepare for liftoff!" Leo announces, holding out the tiny metal bird in the palm of his hand.

"Supercute bird," Becca says.

"It's a drone for aerial surveillance," Leo corrects.

Becca looks confused but I've read about drones in spy articles. Think flying saucer meets toy airplane. They soar overhead like remote controlled planes but are almost invisible tools for covert spying missions.

"I call this a bird-drone," Leo says proudly. "It's a micro-drone since it's so small. If anyone looks up, they'll think it's a bird. But this robotic drone will be recording everything with camera eyes."

So the reflective eyes *are* cameras. Amazing.

"The only drawback," Leo adds, "is that my remote loses control of the bird-drone if it goes beyond sixty-eight yards or stays airborne longer than eleven minutes."

He says "eleven minutes" so precisely that I'm sure that at ten minutes and fifty-nine seconds, the bird will plummet like a rock.

"Coolness," Becca says. "Let's try it out!"

"Over there." I point across the street to Witchy Woman's house. "If we prove she has koi fish, then she's likely the cat dumper too. Maybe she's netted lots of cats and they're all prisoners in her yard."

"Let's find out," Leo says, stepping out of the shade.

He balances the bird-drone on one hand while operating his remote with the other. At the flip of a switch, red lights flash—and blast off. The metal bird seems as light as air as it zooms into the sky like a rocket. Leo explains that the wings turn with a tilt of his lever and the tail whirls like a propeller.

The bird spy-cam zooms higher than tree branches, fluttering in midair while Leo adjusts the directional knob. There's a whirring sound and then the bird-drone soars across the street. I focus to keep the shimmery brown drone in sight as it flies above the Witchy Woman's house. Its wings tilt as it glides over the backyard.

"I bet she has a koi pond," Becca says, hopping excitedly from one sneaker to the other.

"And graves of animal victims," I add gruesomely.

Leo twists a knob on the remote, which I guess is like a steering wheel. "We'll look in other yards too. The camera will record images as it passes over each home."

"I can't wait to see the pictures." I try to follow the bird-drone with my eyes but it blends in the air like a speck of dust. Only its reflective eyes glint when they catch the sun. I blink and lose it for a moment. But there it is again, a tiny glint hovering high over the Witchy Woman's backyard.

"Is it taking photos?" I ask Leo.

Leo nods, frowning at his remote where a light is flashing. He shakes the remote and it rattles then makes a click-clunk noise like a broken toy. The bird-drone soars over the next yard and continues on, moving farther away.

"Shouldn't you bring it back now?" Becca squints into the sky.

Sweat drips down Leo's forehead. "I'm trying."

"What's wrong?" I ask uneasily.

"A minor miscalculation." His voice lacks his usual confidence.

I get a bad feeling. "How minor?" I ask.

"Why won't it respond?" he cries as he struggles with the remote. He presses buttons and flicks switches on the remote.

"You mean it won't come back?"

"Um..." Sweat drips from Leo's brow. "That's a possibility."

"Hit the return button," Becca says.

"There's no return button, it's a combination of...No! This has to work!" He smacks the remote and stomps his foot. "Turn around now!"

But the bird-drone sails away until it's only a twinkle in the distance.

And then it disappears.

- Chapter 12 -
Clue or Coincidence?

"Gone," Leo chokes out the word as if he can't believe he's failed.

"Can't you track it down?" I ask, wondering if I should say something encouraging or eulogize the dead remote control in his hands.

"I could if I'd installed a tracking device—but there wasn't time."

"Oh," is all I can say while Becca pats his arm sympathetically.

"According to my calculations," Leo says in such a devastated tone my heart breaks a little, "it'll fly no farther than .85 miles before it crashes."

I shudder as I imagine the metal bird plummeting to earth and smashing into a zillion pieces. Bye,

bye, bird-drone.

Leo looks pale and queasy like he's going to be sick.

There's nothing else to do except go home.

Drats. We didn't find even one missing pet.

When I get home, Dad has prepared a great dinner, my favorite seafood Alfredo with broccoli. But I hardly taste my food and only halfway listen as my sisters talk about who will or won't ask them to an upcoming school dance. Normally high school dating rituals intrigue me and I listen carefully to discover secrets. But I'm just not in the mood tonight. I go to my room and try to read, which I can't do either since my brain is bouncing with questions.

Will Leo ever see his bird-drone again? Will we find any lost pets? How long can we keep the kittens hidden without anyone finding out? And the biggest mystery—will we discover who dumped them?

And I worry about my family. Everyone pretends that living in this cramped apartment is just fine, but when we talk during dinner it's so fake. Like we're living in a game of pretend, where Dad says, "Everything will be great." And Mom says, "It's so much easier to clean a small apartment." My sisters spend more time away from home with their friends. And my brother is so desperate to win a scholarship, he's always on the computer.

Despite all these worries I'm excited about tomorrow.

I'm getting a tour of Wild Oaks Animal Sanctuary!

After the tour, Becca will introduce me to her mom. Then Becca will show me her room where we'll hang out and bond over our love for animals. We'll have so much fun Becca will want to talk to me more often—even at school.

And (hopefully) we'll become best friends.

I forgot one thing in my plan to become Becca's best friend.

Leo Polanski.

How can Becca and I become besties if he's always with us?

Don't get me wrong—I like Leo a lot. He's super-smart and interesting (when he's not being annoying), and he's an important part of CCSC. But he's too serious—a thinker not a talker. Best friends talk about everything and can practically read each other's minds (which is even cooler than lip-reading). That's what I want with Becca—except she already has the Sparklers.

After school the next day, I head to the Skunk Shack. I've ridden a few blocks when I hear my name and turn to see Leo rolling up on his gyro-board.

"Let's ride together," he says, grinning. "I can't wait to hold an alligator."

"Watch out—or it'll chomp off your fingers," I warn as I shift to a lower gear to bike up the steep hill leading to Becca's property.

"A reptile doesn't scare me," he scoffs.

"Are you afraid of anything?" I ask.

He pauses and looks serious before answering, "Yes." I wait for him to say more, but he doesn't.

Becca is meeting us at her house, so we don't stay long at our clubhouse. Leo feeds the kittens while I refill their water bowl. It's my turn to empty the litter (gross). My kitten finds a loose screw from the broken clock on the floor and bats it around with her claw. The other kittens join in to swat the metal screw like it's a soccer ball. They're so cute, and they're getting more personality every day. Leo's calico (still unnamed) is the smallest in size but fiercest in personality, attacking any bug or shadow that moves. Midnight-black Chris is shy and skittish, hiding at sudden noises. And orange girl Honey purrs the loudest and loves cuddles. I want to take her home so bad. Sigh.

We leave my bike and Leo's gyro-board at the Skunk Shack since we'll stop by later to check on the kittens. We make our way through tall weeds up a craggy hill. When we reach the top, Wild Oaks Animal Sanctuary spreads out below us. I catch my breath, gazing down in awe.

Rustic buildings are surrounded by grassy meadows and towering oaks that must be over a hundred years old. There aren't as many trees in the valley that nestles a sprawling L-shaped home and four outbuildings with high fences and dark moving shapes that I know are animals.

"It's like a hidden community but with more animals than people," I say, marveling at the sprawling property.

"Fifty-six acres," Leo says. And I don't doubt that he's right.

We make our way down a winding path past prickly blackberry bushes with branches that snag my clothes like bony fingers. The closer we get, the larger the buildings seem. The first building we reach is a huge red barn beside a fenced-in pasture. I hear mooing and see a dappled cow grazing with a deer by a water trough where a mallard duck swims.

We pass a building with solar panels and tinted windows. I try to peer inside to see what animals are in there but it's too dark.

Gravel smooths into a paved driveway leading to a blue ranch house with an attached garage bigger than my entire apartment.

An official-looking white truck idles in front of the house and a dark-haired woman who reminds me of Becca leans into its open window. I'm sure the woman is Becca's mother. She's talking to a middle-aged man who's all in brown; his uniform, cap, and even his short hair. I read the printing on the truck: *County Animal Control*.

"Skeet's uncle," Leo guesses, frowning.

Officer Skeet leans out the truck window, smiling at Becca's mom in a friendly, relaxed manner. He seems like a cool guy, but Leo is glaring at him like he's to blame for his nephew's meanness.

I nudge Leo and whisper, "Don't be too quick to judge him. Becca said he entertains sick kids at hospitals and rescued baby ducks."

"He's a Skeet." Leo grits his teeth. "Enough said."

The front door bangs open, and Becca waves as she runs eagerly down the front steps to meet us.

"You made it!" As she hugs me, she whispers, "Is everything okay you-know-where?"

"Per-fect," I say purposely rolling the r like a purr.

She laughs. "I'm glad you came. Come meet my mother," Becca says with a gesture toward the dark-haired woman. "Mom, these are my friends, Leo and Kelsey."

"Always a pleasure to meet Becca's friends," Mrs. Morales says. She turns to the animal control officer who is smiling at us through his open truck window. "This is my friend, Officer Skeet," she says.

"How you doing, kids?" Officer Skeet says in a deep, resonant voice like a TV announcer. He doesn't wait for us to answer, shifting his gaze over to Becca. "How's that pygmy goat coming along?"

"Sinbad's almost weaned," she says proudly. "It wasn't easy to get him to drink from a dish instead of a bottle but I worked with him every day."

"That's what it takes," Officer Skeet says. "I wish that ornery nephew of mine had even half your persistence. Fool kid only wants to play games and slacks off instead of working."

"Um...well," Becca says awkwardly. "He tries."

"I suppose he does." Officer Skeet sighs then pulls his head back into the truck. "Well, I better be on my way. Good to meet you kids. And we'll talk later, Renee."

Exhaust puffs from behind the truck as he starts to back out, but Becca rushes over to the truck. "Wait!" Becca bends toward the open window. "I almost forgot to tell you about the dog."

"Be more specific." Officer Skeet chuckles. "I see lots of dogs."

"The one from the flyer you were passing out. You may not have heard, but Jasper was found and returned to his owner."

"Best news I've heard all day." Officer Skeet taps his hand against the side of the car as if he's keeping in beat with a country song twanging from his radio. "Thanks for letting me know."

An idea strikes me and I step forward. "Officer Skeet, do you have any more lost pet flyers?"

"Why? You starting a collection?" he asks, chuckling.

"No." I feel my cheeks redden. "We ride our bikes a lot and might see other missing pets."

"Good thinking. Too many pets have gone

missing lately." He reaches into his glove box and hands me a bunch of flyers. "Keep a lookout for these pets."

I flip through the flyers, counting eight missing pets. More dogs than cats and most offer rewards. But I don't want to focus on the cash, so I put the two flyers that don't offer rewards on top of the pile.

As Officer Skeet drives away, I remember what Becca said about him raising koi fish on Willow Rose Lane. Of course, owning a koi fish pond doesn't make him a suspect because all the houses on the street have ponds. And if he found kittens, he'd take them to the shelter. He'll know if any of his neighbors have a history of animal abuse—especially Mrs. Tupin.

Mrs. Morales tells Becca she's going to check on an injured goose. "When you go in the house, watch where you step. The fur-bros are loose."

"Fur-bros?" I ask as Becca leads us up the steps and the front door bangs shut behind us.

"You'll see," she says mysteriously.

We walk through an entryway with hooks on one wall for an assortment of coats, hats, and animal leashes. There's a living room on the right and a kitchen on the left. A faded green couch is ripped on one corner like something tried to eat it. There isn't any carpet, only marbled tile that is slick to walk on.

I find out why we need to be careful quickly enough when three gray streaks of fur whoosh past my feet to hide beneath a couch.

"What are those?" I ask.

"Ferret brothers," Becca answers, leading us down a hallway decorated with oil paintings of wild animals. "They're soft and floppy in your hands like furry scarves. Come see my room."

I hurry to catch up with Becca. I can't wait to see her room. She's so creative, I'm sure her room will be gorgeous and reflect her passion for leopard, tiger, and zebra designs.

But when she opens her door, I see a lot of empty space. No carpet or pretty rugs, just plain marbled tile like the rest of the house. No personal things like photos or knickknacks. Just a bed with a fluffy white pillow on a dark-blue comforter, a dresser, a desk, and a chair where two terrier-mix dogs have jumped off to bark excitedly at us.

Becca pets each dog then points. "Look up," Becca says.

"Wow!" I say. "It's like your room is upside down."

All her personal things, like a collage of her life, are plastered like wallpaper to the ceiling: photographs, drawings, letters, report cards, and award certificates. High on the walls, close to the ceiling, are a cork bulletin board, nature paintings, photographs, and award ribbons for showing animals at the country fair. Shelves trail like a road named Becca's Favorite Things, including a shelf of animal books: *Charlotte's Web*, *Freddy the Pig*, *Shiloh*, *Black Beauty*, and *Hank the Cowdog*. A rolling ladder, propped in a corner, gives Becca quick access to her ceiling belongings.

"I got tired of animals chewing my stuff, so I tossed out the old carpet and moved everything out of reach so cats, dogs, and my goat can't ruin them," Becca explains with a gesture to the bed.

Her pillow moves and I jump back with a gasp.

Not a pillow—a tiny, snowy-white goat.

"He's so sweet!" I exclaim. "Can I pet him?"

"Sure. Sinbad loves cuddles."

The tiny goat has floppy ears and pale wavy fur. He's so cute I just want to hug him. But he's sleeping soundly…and snoring.

We pull up chairs and get down to CCSC business.

"Let's sort through the lost pet info," I suggest.

Leo nods. "I can compile location, breeds, dates, and pet descriptions."

"And I'll talk to—" Becca stops when her mother rushes into the room.

"Hurry, Becca!" Mrs. Morales cries, clasping her daughter' hand. "I need your help—the goose's bandage ripped and you're the only one who can hold her still so I can replace it."

Becca's already through the doorway. "I'll be right back," she calls to us.

While we wait, Leo picks up the flyers to read and I climb onto the ladder to look at awards, photos, and paintings. I'm impressed to see Becca's signature on the paintings. I knew she was artistic with her clothes, but still I'm blown away by her painting talent.

I move on to her bulletin board, which is crowded with photos, mostly of her with the Sparklers. There are lots of birthday cards. I glance at the date on one with a chimpanzee hanging upside down from a giant banana. Becca's birthday is in March—just the day after mine. I love having something else in common with her.

I start to climb down until I notice a card that stands out because it's not glittered or pink. It's a photograph of a single blooming rose, hinged open so it's hard not to read the message:

Roses are red.
My eyes are blue.
I hope you like me.
Because I like you.
Will you go out with me again?

It's signed Burt.
(As in Burton Skeet.)

Chapter 13

Wild Times at Wild Oaks

Footsteps clatter from the hall, and I jump away from the wall, plopping onto the bed beside the snoring goat. Becca strides into the room, her cheeks ruddy and her clothes mud-splattered.

"You're wearing a feather," I point out then pluck the smooth white feather from her tiger-striped shirt.

"Feather fashion is très chic," she says in a bad French accent. "I'll weave it into a braid and tell everyone it's the latest style."

"You'll start a new trend." I grin.

"Très magnifique. Everyone will beg me for goose feathers."

"Which you'll sell for a ridiculous amount and make lots of money."

"I'll be rich," Becca says with an airy swish of the feather.

"Great for you—but the poor goose will be naked."

Becca and I giggle and Leo gives us the weirdest look—like he can't figure out what's so funny.

It's easy to joke around with Becca—and I like her more each time we hang out. But a whisper in my brain warns me not to trust her. Becca said she didn't like Skeet, but the card proves she lied.

Skeet wrote, *Will you go out with me again?*

Again? So they've gone out at least once.

How well do I really know Becca? I wonder.

I study her as she playfully dangles the feather near her goat to wake him up. The animal bites at it. Becca has a fun sense of humor and she's a natural with animals. We've been having so much fun today—even Leo is more relaxed, less like a mini-adult and more like a kid. I don't want to ruin the mood by asking about Skeet. It doesn't matter to me if Becca likes him; what matters is that she wasn't honest with me.

"Ready to see the animals?" Becca asks, standing up and leaning against the doorway.

Leo goes over to her. "I've been ready for forty-seven minutes."

"You only care about seeing the alligator," I tease.

"I want to do more than see it." Leo looks at Becca hopefully. "Will you let me hold him?"

Becca shakes her head. "He's small but his teeth are sharp."

Leo makes a humph sound. "I have no intention of being bitten."

"Famous last words," Becca says ominously.

As we tour Wild Oaks, Becca explains that it started as a sanctuary for horses but soon her family was taking in both wild animals and farm animals. The goal is to be a place of refuge for any injured, abused, or abandoned animals. They also educate the public with tours and fund-raising events.

The first stop is a corral that sweeps up to the woods with horses, donkeys, goats, and of course, a zorse. Zed perks his striped ears when I call his name but he continues nibbling his dinner of hay, not at all interested in humans.

I peer into a pen with four massive pigs as Becca pours grain into their trough. They snort and stomp and shove one another with their snouts as they scarf down dinner. Becca explains the different breeds: black-and-white is Hampshire, reddish-brown is Duroc, and the white one is a Yorkshire.

Leo says they stink—which is true—but they're cool anyway.

Behind the pig pen a shallow pond glints with reflected gray clouds. At the center is an island covered with white goo and crowds of birds. Ducks, geese, and even a pair of elegant white swans all seem to be having a party on the island. If Becca really were to get abandoned koi, they could swim here, I think—until a duck dips its beak into the green-gray water and pops back up with a wiggling fish. Okay, not a great place for fish.

We enter a small out-building with a low ceiling and rows of bird eggs warming beneath heat lamps.

"The bird nursery," she explains. "We supply feed stores with baby chicks and other birds, and proceeds help run this place. It was Dad's idea— before he and mom split. They're still really good friends, just not right for each other. Dad is happier living in Seattle. He works for a major IT company but still volunteers here when he's in town."

She pauses like she expects me to share what my father does. But "looking for a job" isn't something I want to talk about, so I point to an open-air enclosure with climbing rocks and ask if we could go there next.

That's when I meet Fuzzy Wuzzy.

"Dumb name for a bear," Leo says.

"It's from an old poem," Becca says then recites:

"Fuzzy Wuzzy was a bear.

"Fuzzy Wuzzy had no hair.

"Fuzzy Wuzzy wasn't very fuzzy.

"Was he?"

I laugh but Leo shakes his head like he thinks we're crazy. And maybe we are, in a good way.

Fuzzy is black but mostly bald with burn scars and random tufts of fur. Even with the scars, he's really cute.

"He was burned in a forest fire that killed his mother," Becca says in a hushed voice as she cradles the cub like a human baby. "He's too injured and gentle to return to the wild, so he'll stay here until a zoo claims him. Here, you hold him."

She hands him to me, and I'm in cuddly bear heaven.

Leo is impatient to see the alligator, but Becca leads us to a rabbit hutch with cages mounted on the wall. Water tubes hang like straws for the bunnies to sip. The cutest rabbit has a mane like a lion, and he's so tiny he fits in my palm. Becca explains how people give cute bunnies to their kids for Easter then decide they're too much work and get rid of them.

Leo runs ahead when he sees the alligator pond.

"Be careful!" Becca warns, hurrying to catch up with him. "Didn't you ever read Peter Pan and learn about dangerous gators? Do you want to wear a hook instead of a hand?"

"Don't be ridiculous," he scoffs. "That was a crocodile."

Still, when Leo gets close to the reptile enclosure, he slows to a stop a few feet from the fence. The alligator is half-submerged in a muddy bathtub that's sunk into the ground. He's only a few feet long, looking more like a log than anything living—until he lifts his head and his yellowy eyes glitter wickedly.

Leo leans cautiously toward the fence. "I thought he'd be bigger," Leo says, sounding disappointed.

"He's only a few months old," Becca says. "But if you offer him your finger, he won't return it."

"I'll watch from here." Leo flexes his fingers and tucks them into his pockets.

"Are you sure? I can get him to come closer so you can touch him."

The alligator swishes his tail and mud sprinkles like raindrops. Leo jumps back, his face pale. "Um, no thanks," Leo says, moving away from the fence.

The last stop of the tour is the dog and cat kennel, where the pens are roomy with soft pet beds. But even the large pens are crowded, so I get why Becca said there isn't room for three kittens.

"These are all foster animals," Becca explains. "Once a week volunteers take them to shopping malls where people can adopt them. But lately, only a few have found homes," she adds as she watches a gray tabby scamper up a climbing post. When Becca sighs I know she's thinking about our kittens, wishing they could be here instead of hidden away.

When we return to Becca's bedroom, we get down to CCSC business. I sit beside Becca on her bed and Leo pulls up a chair.

I hold out the flyers from Officer Skeet. "These will help us recognize missing pets."

"So many lost animals," Becca says sadly as she pets her sleeping goat.

Leo frowns. "It's a crime how people are careless with their pets."

"Yeah, a crime." An idea takes shape in my head and demands attention. "But maybe they aren't being careless."

"I don't get your meaning," Leo says.

I shrug. "Something just feels weird."

"What kind of weird?" Becca asks.

"Weird suspicious." I stare up at the ceiling collage of photos and art, trying to piece together my thoughts. "Too many animals have gone missing in Sun Flower—most of them in the same week. What if they weren't lost?"

Becca's eyes widen. "You don't mean...?"

I nod solemnly. "They were pet-napped."

- Chapter 14 -
Lost and Found

There I said it—the ugly suspicion gnawing at me.

Digging my fingers into the comforter, I wait to hear what Leo and Becca think of my suspicion.

Leo taps his chin like he's considering the idea but Becca is frowning.

"I don't believe it." Becca shakes her head. "Only a few were pedigreed and worth a lot. So why would anyone steal all those pets?"

"I didn't say *all* of them were stolen," I argue. "Just a lot."

"No one needs to steal a pet—our kennel is full of animals no one wants. Most of the missing pets are mixed breeds, not purebreds worth lots of money." Becca taps her finger on a flyer with a photo of a scruffy mixed-breed terrier. "Why would anyone steal a dog that is half-blind and sixteen years old."

"That's 112 years old in dog years," Leo says.

"Not even the dumbest pet thief in the world would steal an old, blind dog," Becca points out. "Besides, the flyer says that dog wandered off because a gate was left open. Kelsey, I know you like mysteries, but animals get lost all the time. This is not a mystery."

I want to argue but she sounds so logical that I doubt myself.

It's a surprise when Leo takes my side. "According to my calculations," he says, "factoring in the estimated population of Sun Flower with the ratio of missing reports, the percentage of lost pets is high."

I glance at Becca to see if this convinces her but she just looks confused.

"Let's just focus on helping animals," Becca says with a sigh. "Whether they're lost or stolen, they need to be found."

"By the CCSC," Leo adds.

"Want to go out riding tomorrow?" I ask. But they both shake their heads. Leo has flute practice and Becca doesn't say what she's doing, just that she can't make it. We agree to go pet-hunting the day after.

We aren't in a hurry to leave, so we pass around the papers and talk about missing pets. Becca scans and prints each flyer so we all have our own copies.

Leo perches himself on a high step of the ladder, his loafers dangling in the air while he reads through the papers. I lean over Becca's shoulder, reading along with her. The terriers are curled on the bed too and the smallest climbs into my lap. I scratch beneath his chin as I memorize each photo so the next time I spot a missing animal like the gray cat, I'll be ready.

We're all so quiet, the loudest noise coming from the snoring goat, when Leo suddenly shouts. "A map!" He jumps down from the ladder with a thump, scattering Becca's flyers over the floor. "I need a map."

"Why?" Becca asks as she picks up her papers.

"To map out the locations where pets have gone missing," Leo explains. "May I use your computer?"

"Sure," Becca says, gesturing toward her desk.

As he prints out a map of Sun Flower, he tells Becca, "I need pushpins, multicolored."

Becca opens a desk drawer, fumbles around, and then drops pins into Leo's waiting hand. He tacks the map onto Becca's bulletin board and sticks a colored pushpin onto the map for each missing pet: red for dogs, blue for cats, and green for other animals. When Leo's finished, pushpins trail a rainbow of lost pets across Sun Flower—even in the exclusive communities with security gates, where pets should have been protected.

"Nine dogs, five cats, a goat, and a pig," Leo says, tapping each location to match the missing pet. "I'm looking for a pattern, but animals have been lost all over Sun Flower."

"The pig disappeared downtown." I walk over to the map and point to a green pushpin. "Wouldn't someone notice a pig wandering around businesses?"

"I would," Leo says.

"The pig could be back home by now," Becca says. "Just because we have a flyer doesn't mean the pet is still lost."

"Let's find out by calling the owners," I suggest.

Becca reaches for her cell phone but Leo shakes

his head and offers his phone. "It's programmed to record and auto-transcribe."

"You record conversations?" I ask, wondering if that's even legal.

"I've never had a reason to—before now." His blue eyes shine eagerly. "As Covert Technology Strategist, I have the latest hi-tech."

"Coolness." Becca smiles as she takes his phone. "I'm the CCSC Social Contact Operative so I'll make the calls."

"And my role as Spy Tactics Specialist is to analyze info," I add, proud to sound official. "I'll take notes. Let's call about the pig first."

I read the flyer while Becca calls.

Two-year-old male potbellied pig, dark-brown, friendly, $50 reward.

"Hi, I'm calling about your pig," Becca begins and then nods as she listens.

I perch on the edge of the bed beside Becca, straining my ears. But all I can hear is Becca saying, "Oh...uh-huh...really?"

When she finally clicks off, I jump at her. "What did you find out?"

"Good and weird news."

"Weird news first," I say.

Leo shrugs. "The order of news has little bearing on the information."

"Well, the pig was returned—that's the good news." Becca reaches to pet the two dogs curled on the floor by her feet. "Then it gets weird because guess who returned the pig?"

I arch my brows curiously. "Who?"

Becca grins. "Santa Claus."

"An early Christmas gift," I play along with her joke. "I wouldn't want to gift wrap a pig."

"The hooves would rip the paper." Becca taps the pointy hooves on her snoring goat.

"Santa did *not* return a pig," Leo insists. "That's impossible."

"I'm only repeating what I was told," Becca says in a serious tone, but I catch the twinkle in her eyes. "I guess the guy looked just like Santa, from snowy beard to black boots. She called him Santa, and I wasn't going to argue with her. So what's the next phone number?"

I read off the number for a female dachshund.

This call takes less than a minute. When Becca clicks the phone off, she reports the dog was found. "He was returned the same day," she adds.

"Wow." I whistle softly. "That was quick."

"A mechanic found him rooting in the garbage behind an auto repair shop." Becca looks over my shoulder as I cross off the dachshund from my list.

"What did the mechanic look like?" I ask because a good spy gathers all the information.

"She didn't say his age or anything, just that he had spider tattoos on his arms."

I write down mechanic and spider tattoos then close my file.

When I glance at a tiger-shaped wall clock, I'm surprised it's already after five. I have to leave soon, so we hurry through the rest of the calls. Five don't answer. Of the eleven we do reach, four pets are still missing but eight were returned—three by a guy with spider tattoos.

"The same guy returned three pets?" I say, reading my notes to make I hadn't made a mistake.

"He must be really good at finding pets," Becca says.

"Or it's a coincidence," I say.

"There are no coincidences, only patterns." Leo taps his fingers on the print-outs. "The dog was only lost for a few hours and the cat was returned the next day. And didn't that girl, Emma, say her friend's dog was returned by a tattooed guy?"

"Could it be the same guy?" I wonder, skimming through my notes. "Three—maybe four—pets returned within a few days. Spider Tattoo works fast."

"He's not the only one." Leo reads through the flyers, a crease deepening in his forehead. "Two of the dogs were returned by an old guy with a white beard. Who does that sound like?"

"Santa," Becca and I answer.

"And when I called about Jasper, he was returned by an old woman with a cane." I check my notes. "And the Chihuahua was also found by an old woman."

"A pattern emerges," Leo says as he skims through his flyers. "All owners offering a reward had their pets returned within twenty-four hours. But the four owners who didn't offer rewards are still missing their pets."

"Someone is stealing pets for the rewards!" Becca cries out in outrage.

"Not *someone*," I say with a grim check of my notes. "Spider Tattoo, Santa, and an old woman. It's a whole crime ring of pet-nappers."

- Chapter 15 -
Secrets and Lies

That night, I toss and turn and punch my pillow. I always wanted to spy to uncover secrets but what started as a search for a cat-dumper just exploded into a crime spree.

Stealing innocent animals to con people out of money is cruel. Losing a pet is heartbreaking—even for a few hours. I feel terrible for the four non-reward pets that are still missing. There could be more too, but we won't know until we can talk to all the owners.

As I read through the flyers, I'm more certain than ever that the three dogs and cat that are still missing won't be returned unless their owners offer a reward. But what if the owners can't afford it? Will their pets ever come home?

I think of my own dog. I miss Handsome sooo much. I've been so busy with the CCSC I haven't visited Gran Nola in over a week. I plan to visit tomorrow since there's no club meeting. Leo has flute practice and Becca has plans too—though she said she'd find time to feed the kittens.

Plans with who? I wonder. Her parents, the Sparklers, or Skeet?

I ball up my pillow and try to sleep on my side but that doesn't feel right so I roll onto my back. Moonlight slices through my blinds, casting silvery stripes across my ceiling. The stripes make me think of Becca's animal print outfits. I think about how exciting it was to rescue the zorse and then find out Becca knew my name. I thought we've been getting close—but she lied to me about Skeet.

Why didn't she trust me with the truth? I don't care if she's going out with him; it's the lying that hurts.

Club members—and future best friends—should trust each other.

Since I can't sleep, I toss off my blankets and cross the room to the carved wooden chest beneath my window. The decorative molding on the bottom of the chest hides a camouflaged drawer that's the perfect place to keep my deepest secrets.

I pull out my notebook of secrets.

I started the list in fifth grade after a sleepover at Ann Marie's house when I accidentally overheard her mother tell her aunt that she was getting a divorce. I was shocked and worried about Ann Marie. She thought her parents were happy together. Only I knew they were protecting her and waiting for a trip to Disneyland to break the news.

So I knew this huge secret but I couldn't tell anyone. If I told Ann Marie, she'd hate me for finding out before her. And if I told anyone else, it would be a betrayal to Ann Marie. But this secret was like an alien trapped inside my head screaming to get out.

So I tucked the secret safely between the pages of a plain blue notebook, burying it in my hidden drawer, planning never to look at it again.

But something unexpected happened—I discovered more secrets. I didn't mean to eavesdrop at first. Curiosity took over and I started snooping on purpose. Now, I have over a dozen pages of secrets.

I flip to a new page and write:

BECCA MORALES: She's gone out with Skeet but says she doesn't like him. Why did she lie to me? Does she actually like him or is he blackmailing her into dating him? Can I trust her? More research needed.

Becca isn't at school the next day. I ask about her in the office, and a student assistant says she called in sick. How sick? I want to contact her to see if she's okay, but I don't have a phone. Leo does though, and I know he'd let me use it. Only we agreed to keep our friendship a secret at school. But it can't hurt to talk to him just for a minute, right?

Leo is sitting in his usual spot at lunch, drawing on his tablet with an intent look, totally lost in his thoughts. I stare at the back of his blond hair and mentally command him to look at me. But he doesn't stop drawing. A tornado could whip the roof off over his head and he still wouldn't look up.

Frustrated, I head over to my usual table with Ann Marie and Tori.

As I pass Becca's table, I glance at her chair, expecting it to be empty.

But it isn't—and I *cannot* believe who's sitting in her place.

What is that Red-Ponytail-Means-Trouble jerk doing with the Sparklers? Not just sitting with them, but *flirting!* Laughing, he leans close to Sophia and puts his arm around her. Seriously, does Skeet have no loyalty? How can he write a love poem to Becca then hit on her friends?

If Becca really likes him, she's going to be hurt.

But only if someone tells her. And I can't hurt her like that.

Add another secret to add to my list, I think with a sigh.

After school, I bike home instead of going to the Skunk Shack, which feels strange. Mom doesn't even notice when I enter the living room. She's focused on the computer, frowning as she scrolls through an official-looking website. Before she knows I'm there, I peer over her shoulder because I'm naturally snoopy.

"You're looking for a job!" I say, which startles her so much she whirls around and bumps her shoulder into my elbow.

"*Ow!*" I cry, holding my elbow.

"Kelsey!" Mom rubs her shoulder. "I've told you not to sneak up on me."

"I wasn't sneaking. I was reading over your shoulder. So what's with the job listings? I thought you liked working at the florist shop."

"Well, since you must know everything," Mom says sternly but with a smile, "I do like my job but it's time for a change."

"And a job working for the county would pay more," I say.

"That too."

"Only you won't be as happy. You love working with flowers."

"You're too smart for my own good." Mom reaches out to muss my hair. "So what are you doing home anyway? I thought you were glued to your new friends."

"They're busy."

"And you're feeling left out?" Mom guesses with a raised brow.

"Now who's the one who's too smart?" I retort.

"Friendships aren't easy—no matter what age you are," Mom says, squeezing my hand gently. "Sometimes I worry you're too quiet. Be open and honest with your friends."

Honest? I think about Becca. *How can I be honest with a liar?*

Still, Mom has a point. It's easier for me to listen than talk. I'm so used to spying on people who seem more interesting than me. But since joining CCSC, I'm doing interesting stuff too. And I've gained two great friends.

I realize I shouldn't judge Becca. Who she dates is not up to me, and I'll try not to care if she likes a boy I dislike. I'll tell her she's the nicest girl I've ever met and admit I'm tired of pretending not to like her at school. And I'll ask her if we can be best friends.

After dinner, while I'm rinsing off dirty dishes, my parents call a family meeting. I shut off the tap and hurry into the living room.

My stomach knots because the last time we had a family meeting, my parents broke the bad news of losing our house.

I'm tense when I enter the living room—until I see who's there.

"Gran Nola!" I rush over and fall into a soft hug. Gran Nola, my mother's mom, is short like me but athletic from cycling in competitions and teaching yoga.

Gran has Handsome with her. My gorgeous golden whip barks excitedly and wags his tail so fast that when I bend down to hug him he almost knocks over a lamp. Dad catches it before it hits the floor. My sisters and brother crowd around Handsome, and we're all hugging our dog.

Not a family meeting—a family party!

We celebrate with a game of Monopoly.

"I'm going to break the bank," Dad says, rubbing his hands together like a villain threatening to take over the world.

"Not if I send you to jail first," Gran threatens.

And the game is on!

We roll dice and laugh and argue—until Kyle buys up the last property and bankrupts everyone.

When Dad brings out red velvet cupcakes for dessert, we're all winners.

Saying good-bye to Gran and Handsome is hard, but I'm still smiling as I go to bed. And I sleep great.

The next day at school, Becca is back and she's looks gorgeous in a striped skirt, leather ankle boots, and a scalloped leather jacket over a white blouse. I admire the golden tiger necklace shining around her neck. She's straightened her dark hair so it falls smoothly down her back.

Although we're still keeping our friendship a secret at school, in homeroom she turns around to whisper, "See you at the shack."

After school, I reach the Skunk Shack a few minutes before Becca joins me. Leo isn't there yet— he texted Becca to say he'd be late.

"I was worried about you yesterday," I tell Becca as I reach for a can of cat food. There are only three cans left.

"Worried?" She looks over at me curiously as she fills a water bowl.

"I heard you were sick."

"Oh...that." Her cheeks redden. "I wasn't actually sick. I told Mom I needed a no-stress day to do some thinking."

"And she let you stay home?" I'm stunned. I have to be burning up with fever or vomiting before my parents let me miss school.

"Mom can be bossy, and lately we argue a lot, but we work hard to keep Wild Oaks running so she's more like a partner than a parent. She trusts me to make my own decisions," Becca says. "But figuring out the right decisions isn't easy. There's a lot to think about."

"About what?" *Be honest with me,* I silently urge.

"Nothing to do with the club."

"Maybe I can help anyway," I persist. "I'm good at keeping secrets. You can trust me."

"I can, can't I?" She looks closely at me like maybe she's realizing she really can trust me.

And I want so badly to trust her...

Wheels whirl from outside and I hear Leo shout, "Becca! Kelsey! Wait till you see what I have."

I groan. His timing couldn't be worse.

"We'll talk later," Becca says, squeezing my hand.

We step outside the shack just as Leo hops off his gyro-board.

He's breathing hard and sweating but grinning. "I found it!" he says.

"What's going on?" I ask.

He waves something small in the air like a winning trophy.

The bird-drone is back.

We go into the Skunk Shack and pull up our chairs to the table. I spot a cobweb on the ceiling and dust on the window ledge like nature is trying to reclaim our clubhouse.

Leo sets the bird-drone on the table where it teeters on its spiky metal legs—until one snaps off and rolls onto the floor. The kittens pounce after this strange new toy. Normally I'd smile at their playfulness but we're all staring sadly at Leo's smashed robot. The bird-drone wobbles on one leg then flops onto its side with a plunk.

"Poor busted bird." Becca sighs like the drone is a living creature.

Poor Leo, I think. He was so proud when his bird-drone lifted off into the sky. "Can you fix it?"

"Doubtful." Leo shakes his head. "It was badly damaged in the crash."

"How did you find it without a tracking device?" I ask.

"I calculated the flight pattern and distance, then narrowed the search area to a baseball field. It smashed down on third base. A sad end for a fine robot." He bows his head.

"You can make another one," Becca encourages, reaching out to squeeze his hand. "You're really smart."

"Thanks," Leo says with a pained smile. "At least the bird-drone did its job before it crashed."

"What do you mean...ouch!" Claws dig into my ankle. I look down to see my playful orange kitten. I scoop her up and she purrs as I hug her.

"It flew over Willow Rose Lane and took nineteen photos," Leo is saying. "By cross-checking with Google maps, I matched the addresses to the photos."

"You got photos of the backyards?" I ask eagerly.

Leo unzips the leather pouch he carries instead of a backpack and pulls out a large envelope. "Check these out."

Becca leans in beside me, her tiger necklace brushing my shoulder as we look through the photos. Most of them are distant aerial views of rooftops, driveways with shiny cars, and backyards with green lawns, bricked patios, barbecues, gardens, sheds, and garages. But the last three photos are close-ups of ponds with glittering water and rainbow swirls of fish.

"I zoomed in on those photos because of the ponds," Leo explains.

"Koi fish!" I point excitedly.

"So pretty—like jewels swimming in rainbows," Becca says. "I'd love to have koi at Wild Oaks."

"So would your alligator," I tease. "Chomp, chomp. Sushi."

She swats at me. "You're terrible."

"It's a talent," I say, grinning.

Leo is all seriousness as he plucks three photos from the pile and spreads them on the table. "All the houses have ponds but only three have koi fish."

"Who owns the—no kitty! Don't eat the photos." I gently put Honey on the floor where she scampers after her siblings.

"Mrs. Tupin lives in the house with koi fish," Leo says.

"This proves she's guilty!" I snap my fingers. "Witchy Woman dumped our kittens."

"Actually it only proves she has koi fish," Leo says. "Don't forget the receipt you found also listed dog and cat food."

"She could have a dog and cat inside her house," I say stubbornly. "Becca and I think she might own the mother cat but didn't want to the kittens, so she got rid of them."

"Interesting theory." Leo taps his chin thoughtfully. "That would explain where the kittens came from."

"And tossed them away in a plastic bag like trash." Becca scowls.

"Leo, who lives in this house?" I point to one with a barbecue patio with potted plants, wicker chairs, and koi fish swimming in a pond with a waterfall.

"The Stanfords—a retired couple. I recognized the name because their granddaughter is in my fencing class."

"So did you call her?" I ask.

"Why waste time talking on the phone when there's more info online? I searched their social media posts and found out they travel a lot and have been on vacation for a month. They have a dog that travels with them."

"Who feeds their fish?" Becca asks, always worrying about pets.

"A neighbor," he answers in a precise way like he's reading off a list but he isn't. "And this pond with the lion statue is Officer Skeet's."

"We already know he has koi fish," Becca says in a defensive tone.

I'm more interested in Witchy Woman's yard. A chain-link fence surrounds a small slanted roof. Could it be a dog house? I don't see a dog but he could be sleeping inside. I check off each piece of evidence in my notebook:

a) dog pen

b) koi fish

c) possibly owns Mama Cat

"Witchy Woman is so guilty," I say. "All we need to do is prove she has Mama Cat."

"How do we prove it?" Becca asks.

"Talk to the neighbors," Leo suggests, lifting his gaze from the photos to us. "Someone will know if she has a cat—especially a cat who had kittens. According to my calculations, one kitten in a litter will resemble its mother."

"That does happen a lot." Becca bends down to pet her kitten. "So the mother cat will be black like Chris, orange like Honey, or calico like No-Name. You really have to name your kitten, Leo."

"Why name a cat I can never have? Dad will always be allergic." Leo frowns as he watches the three kittens playing. "Let's focus on catching the cat-dumper. We need to find out if Mrs. Tupin owns the mother cat."

"If she still has it," I say ominously as I study the photo again, looking beyond the dog pen.

A far corner blooms with flowers—except for a square of dirt. I peer closer at the photo and what I see sends shivers up my skin. "Look at the dirt by the fence." I point. "It's fresh and dark like someone's been digging…burying something small."

Becca gasps. "What are you saying?"

"That I know what happened to the kitten's mother." I point to the photo. "There's her grave."

- Chapter 17 -

Spies and Lies

The CCSC is in stealth spy mode. We wheel around Willow Rose Lane three times before meeting up under our usual shady willow tree.

"Witchy Woman's black SUV isn't in the driveway," I say, peering through willow vines. "I think she isn't home."

"Looks like it," Becca agrees. "The blinds are usually open but they're closed now."

"Excellent," Leo says with a determined glint in his blue eyes. "I'll search the backyard. If she has a cat—dead or alive—I'll find it."

"No." I shake my head firmly. "That's too dangerous."

"Someone might see you," Becca warns.

"And what about the dog?" I add with a frown at the photo in my hand. "Just because he's not in the photo doesn't mean he isn't there."

"The worst he'll do is bark, and if he does, I can run fast." Leo kicks up his gyro-board and hands me the remote. "Watch this for me."

Leo suddenly seems taller and less geeky. Bravery looks good on him, I think with surprise. But he can't be serious. Climb a fence in pressed slacks and a button-down dress shirt? He'll end up flat on his butt.

Becca and I offer to go with him but he says we should keep watch and text if Witchy Woman shows up. Becca holds her phone so we're ready as we spy half-hidden beneath wispy willow vines.

Even in loafers instead of sneakers, Leo bolts over the gate like a gymnast. Becca bites her lip and my heart thuds so loudly it's all I can hear. I imagine everything that can go wrong. Leo will trip and break his leg. He'll fall into the fish pond and drown. There really is a vicious dog and it's very hungry. Or Witchy Woman really is a witch and she's lurking in her house ready to grab Leo, and we'll never see him again.

Six minutes...eight minutes...twelve. What's taking Leo so long?

"Hey, Becca!" a male voice shouts.

Becca shrieks and I jump so high I hit my head on a willow branch. We spin around as Burton Skeet rolls up on a black bike.

"What are you doing here, Bec? You don't live around here." He's grinning at her in a sappy way that makes me want to puke.

"Just riding around," Becca says uneasily.

Skeet jerks his thumb at me. "With *her*?"

He says "her" like I'm something gross you scrap off from the bottom of your shoe. But he's taller with muscles, so I don't argue.

"I can hang out with whoever I want. And Kelsey and I are busy, so just leave," Becca says sharply. Unlike me, she has no fear of Skeet.

"Busy doing what?" He narrows his eyes.

"None of your business."

"Don't snap at me, Bec," he says in a softer tone. "You'll hurt my feelings."

Does Skeet have feelings? I wonder, backing up close to my bike in case I need a quick getaway.

"Just go home," she tells him.

"I will if you come with me." He gives her this little-boy grin, all flashy white teeth and dimples. I have to admit he's good-looking. But

I know beneath the grin lurks a viper ready to strike.

"Don't be crazy." Becca purses her lips like she's trying not to lose her temper. "We can talk later."

"Or now." He dips his head close to her face, "I've missed you, Bec."

"Burt, please...this isn't a good time." Becca looks panicked like a trapped animal as she glances from me to Skeet. "I'll call you tonight if you leave."

His gaze slithers over me. "You didn't tell me what you're doing with her. She's not a Sparkler."

I watch Becca, urging her to say I'm her friend.

"I'm helping Kelsey find...find her dog," Becca turns toward me and mouths, "Play along."

"You lost a dog?" Skeet asks, suddenly interested. "That sucks. I could help you look. You probably know that my uncle is an animal control officer. I help him out a lot."

I remember Officer Skeet complaining that Burt was lazy and not very helpful, but I keep quiet.

"So go help him," Becca says. "We can find the dog on our own."

But Burton Skeet doesn't move. "Is there a reward?"

I say yes just as Becca says no.

"Kelsey was thinking about offering a reward but we're sure we'll find him," Becca improvises.

"You'll find him quicker with my help," Skeet persists.

I grip my handlebars so tight my knuckles turn white. Things only get worse when I look across the street and spot Leo halfway over the fence.

Oh no! It'll be a disaster if Skeet sees Leo.

I catch Becca's gaze and mouth Leo's name and point. She glances across the street and her eyes pop with panic.

"Burt, you have to go!" Becca nudges Skeet so his view of the street is blocked by a curtain of vines. "You can't help because Kelsey's dog is... um...afraid of guys. He'll run if he sees you with us. So you have to go."

"Is that any way to treat me after what I gave you?"

"That was sweet." Becca twirls her finger in the gold chain of the tiger necklace. "It's really pretty."

"I knew you'd like it." He grins, dimples making him dangerously attractive.

"Okay, I like it. But you need to leave or we'll never catch the dog."

While she's talking to Skeet, I'm watching Leo. He can't see through the willow branches, so he has no idea Skeet is here. Leo looks left then right at the neighboring houses before moving away from the fence. I hold my breath as he creeps low, staying near bushes. Once he crosses the street, he'll be in plain view.

"I'll go on one condition," Skeet tells Becca with a sly grin.

"What?" She bites her lip.

Skeet bends over and whispers in her ear. I can't hear what he says but I can read his lips, and what I read makes me want to vomit.

I'm sure Becca will push him away or slap him. But she doesn't even look outraged. And she's blushing.

She looks over at me and mouths, "Sorry."

Then Becca lifts her face to Skeet's and kisses him.

- Chapter 18 -
Accusations

I've never seen a bigger smile than Skeet's as he hops back onto his bike. He's whirling away while I'm still reeling. The good news is I don't spew chunks. But the bad news is I'm so shocked I can hardly think straight. Please let this be a hallucination.

But it really happened. OMG!

Becca kissed the guy she told me she wanted to avoid; the same guy who gave her a romantic poem and a necklace; the guy I'm beginning to think she likes more than she wants to admit—even to herself.

"Don't hate me," Becca whispers.

"I don't...but how could you?"

"I—I don't know. It seemed like a good idea."

"Kissing someone like Skeet is never a good idea. Yuck."

"I got him to leave, didn't I?" she asks as if proud of herself.

"But you shouldn't have let him blackmail you. That's disgusting. You must have heard how horrible he was to Leo."

"Rumors get exaggerated. He's never mean around me so it's hard to believe things I've heard about him. Still, Leo won't understand so he can't know about this." She clasps my hand. "Promise you won't tell him."

I nod, adding another secret to my collection.

I may need to start a new notebook soon.

Still, I can hardly believe Becca kissed Skeet. She's not afraid of him, so why didn't she tell him to get lost? Was she really trying to protect Leo? Or did she kiss Skeet because she wanted to?

When Leo sprints across the street to join us, he's out of breath but grinning. "That was such a rush!"

"Tell me about it," I mutter with a dark look at Becca.

"You were very brave." Becca smiles at him, turning away from me.

"I was, wasn't I?" Leo puffs up proudly and looks down at his white shirt, which isn't so white anymore. "Did you see me climb the fence and then jump back down? I felt like I was flying like a drone." Leo waves his arms. "Spying is exciting."

"It can be dangerous too, if you're not careful," I warn.

"According to my calculations, the danger risk was only seventeen percent. And wait till you hear what I found out!"

I glance up then down the street, worried Skeet might return. "Let's go somewhere more private to talk."

"The Skunk Shack?" Becca suggests.

"My apartment is closer," I say. "Although it won't be private if my family is home."

"The decision is obvious." Leo jumps onto his gyro-board. "We'll go to my house. It's the closest, and I have no siblings—only an aquarium of very quiet fish."

Becca and I pedal fast to keep up with Leo, so we don't talk—which is a good thing since I'm afraid of what I might say. I can't stop thinking about that kiss. I feel like I don't even know Becca. How can someone so smart kiss a boy like Skeet? I just don't understand.

"My parents are working but we still have to follow the no-shoes rule." Leo holds the front door open then gestures for us to sit on a carved wood bench in the foyer. "Mom doesn't allow shoes on the carpet."

"Wow, your house is all white on the inside too," I say as I untie my sneakers. White walls and snowy carpet, and even the wall paintings are of snowy mountains and milky-foam ocean waves.

"It's embarrassing," Leo admits with a cringe. "But I'm used to it. And she let me choose the colors for my own room. It's the one at the end of the hall."

Leo's room is huge—more like a suite. It has a private bath and a living room with a flat-screen TV and shelves overflowing with plastic containers of tools and electronic parts. There's even a life-size robot standing in a corner like a prop from a science fiction movie.

Leo clicks a remote and the robot-man's chest hinges open like wings unfolding to reveal a large screen.

"Is that another TV?" Becca asks.

"No, it's my computer. Check out the photos I took while I was in Mrs. Tupin's backyard," he says as he connects his phone to the robot computer.

Becca stands on one side of Leo and I move to the other. I catch her looking at me curiously but I look away. Now that my shock is over, anger has taken its place. Can I believe anything she tells me?

Leo seems oblivious to the tension between Becca and me. He taps his keyboard then points at the screen. "There's the fenced-in dog pen."

"But no dog," Becca says, disappointed.

"The pen clearly hasn't been used in a long time." Leo clicks to a new photo. "Here's the patch of fresh dirt that Kelsey spotted."

"A grave," I say in a hush, leaning closer to the screen. "There's something poking up from the dirt. Is it a stick?"

"Maybe a flag," Becca adds.

"Or a headstone," I say ominously.

"You were closer when you guessed a stick." Leo clicks a few buttons and the screen in the robot's chest focuses on the fresh dirt. "It's a rose plant."

"Like flowers on a grave?" I shiver and think of the missing mother cat.

"Wrong again," he says with that know-it-all grin that annoys me. "That rose bush was just planted. No flowers yet, only thorny branches. Definitely *not* a grave. Mrs. Tupin is a gardener with blooming flowers all over her yard. But no signs of a dog or cat."

"A house cat?" I guess.

Leo shakes his head. "I looked in the windows and saw no evidence of any indoor pets."

"Drats. I was so sure Witchy Woman dumped the kittens." Frowning, I turn away form the computer. "We just ran out of suspects."

I'd been so sure the receipt was a great clue. It was in the same bag as the kittens, so it must have belonged to the cat dumper. But of the three people with koi fish, Witchy Woman is the most likely suspect. The Stanfords are on vacation so they obviously didn't do it. And an animal control officer has no reason to dump kittens when he can easily take them to the shelter.

What if no one on Willow Rose Lane is guilty? The cat-napper could have koi fish in a different neighborhood. Or I might have the right neighborhood but the wrong suspects. Maybe it's not someone who lives in one of these houses but someone who visits often—like a nephew who helps out his uncle.

Would helping include buying pet food?

"Becca," I say carefully, "remember when we found the kittens?"

"Of course," she answers in a wary voice.

"We wouldn't have found them if we hadn't detoured through the alley, and we only did that because you wanted to avoid someone."

She presses her lips together tightly. "So?"

"It means he was near the alley," I say with emphasis on *alley*. "Did you ever wonder what he was doing there?"

"No." She flips back her dark hair defiantly. "And you shouldn't either."

"What's going on with you two?" Leo spins around in his computer chair. "Who are you talking about?"

I ignore Leo, staring hard at Becca. She reminds me of a timid deer, ready to leap away if I come to close to a suspicion she doesn't want to hear.

"Drop it, Kelsey," she warns, folding her arms across her chest.

"Don't you find it suspicious that not only was he near the alley where the kittens were dumped, but he also spends time with his uncle who lives on

Willow Rose Lane and has koi fish? He probably has dogs and cats too."

Leo jumps out of his chair to face us. "Are you talking about Skeet?"

"Kelsey, drop it." Becca narrows her gaze. "I don't want to talk about him."

"But you didn't mind *kissing* him?"

Oops. As soon as I say it, I know I've gone too far.

Leo's mouth falls open. "You—you kissed Skeet?"

"Kelsey!" Becca's cheeks blaze. "You promised not to tell!"

"You *kissed* Skeet? Actually pressed your lips against his?" Leo holds on to the top of his chair as if his legs have gone weak.

"It's not how you think…" When Leo won't look at her, she whirls back to me. "I can't believe you told him! I thought I could trust you!"

"Trust?" I repeat the word bitterly. "You're the one who lied. You said you didn't like Skeet but you've gone out with him and he even gave you that necklace you're wearing."

"You don't understand," she says looking close to tears.

"No, I don't. How can you like a boy cruel enough to dump helpless kittens?"

"He didn't do it!" she argues.

"Yes, he did—it all makes sense," I say, excited as the clues fall into place. "Skeet was close to the dumpster, his uncle has koi fish, and he's mean. Move him up to Suspect number one."

"You think you're so smart," Becca snaps. "But you're wrong."

"Kelsey made some excellent points," Leo says.

"Are you siding with her?" Becca wheels on Leo, hands in fists.

"No...I mean..." Leo stammers.

"I am so out of here." Becca storms over to the door and yanks it open.

"Don't leave," I say, softening my voice. "Let's talk it over."

"There's nothing to talk about—you won't listen."

"I always listen!"

"Only to what you want to hear." Becca turns furiously toward me. "You called me a liar. I thought being in a club meant trusting each other. Guess I was wrong."

"Becca, I'm trying to trust you," I tell her honestly.

"But you don't," she accuses. "So we're done. And don't worry about the kittens. Mom told me about a new volunteer who wants to foster cats. I wasn't going to tell Mom about our kittens but it's not like we can keep them anyway. The kittens will be in a good home until they can be adopted. There's no reason for either of you to come back to the Skunk Shack."

She slams the door, the bang loud and final.

The CCSC is over.

- Chapter 19 -
Cat-Tastrophe

I can't believe it   one moment we're having a great
time working together, then all a sudden it's over.
No friendship. No kittens. No club.

I blink back tears, trying hard not to cry in
front of Leo. His face looks stunned like a grenade
exploded in his room. That's how I feel too. Becca's
words blasted away the CCSC.

"I have to go," I say miserably.

"Of course you do." He's quiet as he follows me
to the front door.

"Sorry about…about everything." I sit on the
ornate bench. I bend over to slip on a sneaker, rubbing off a spot of dirt on the toe.

"It's not your fault. I expected something like

this to happen."

"You knew Becca would quit on us?" I ask in astonishment as I look up at him, a shoe string dangling through my fingers.

"No, not that." He moves toward the door, holding it open for me.

But I don't leave, slowly tying the other shoe. When I stand, I place my hand on his arm. "Leo, what do you mean?"

Light shines through the open door, partly on Leo's face so he's half in brightness and half in shadow. "According to my calculations, friendship never ends well...for me anyway." He sucks in a heavy breath then blows it out. "Remember when you asked if I was afraid of anything?"

"You said yes. But you didn't tell me your fear."

"Fears are the result of imagining the worst that can happen. I am too logical for fears. This doesn't mean I'm brave—far from it. I simply lack common fears like heights, public speaking, or snakes." He swallows. "But since joining CCSC, I've been afraid it will end. And now it has."

"Oh, Leo." I reach out and squeeze his hand. "I'm you're friend, and Becca is too."

He gives me this thin smile, like he knows I mean

well, but he also knows the club is what made us friends. I should say I'll sit with him at lunch or go to his house after school. And that I'll want to hang out with him...but I probably won't.

So I say good-bye and leave.

I dream about kittens that night.

I'm in a dark endless house with twisting corridors leading nowhere. I hear mews, but I can't see any cats. I wander from room to room, calling for my kitten. Are you there, Honey? Where are you hiding? Why can't I find you? I see the swish of an orange tail and race after it. "Wait!" I shout but the furry tail whips around a corner. When I finally get close enough to grab it, there's a ferocious growl. I'm holding a tiger's tail...

It's a relief to wake up...until I think of my kitten. Alone in my room, I cry.

I'm spending Saturday with Gran Nola and Handsome. Gran makes caramel popcorn pancakes for brunch then we watch episodes of our favorite mystery shows like *Bones* and *Veronica*

Mars. When Gran gets a call from one of her yoga clients, I go into the backyard and play Frisbee fetch with Handsome. It's no accident his name is Handsome—his fur glistens like gold and his eyes shine like black gems. It's great to be with him again, but it makes me miss my kitten even more.

After Frisbee exhausts both of us, Handsome snoozes on the ground beneath me while I sway gently in the shaded hammock. Gran planted the maple trees that support the hammock when I was born, so it's like being cradled by old friends. My mind sways like the hammock, drifting back to a hidden shack in the woods and the kittens that are no longer there.

I don't want to think about the kittens so I dig into my backpack for the mystery novel I started reading last week—before CCSC. I grab the edge of a paperback, but when I pull it out it's not a book. It's my Pet Project Folder. I start to toss it back but change my mind.

Becca quit the club—I didn't. We can't take care of the kittens in the Skunk Shack anymore but I can still look for lost pets.

I lean back in the hammock and read through the

folder, memorizing descriptions of missing pets. I cross-reference the map of Sun Flower and realize that one of the lost dogs, a female cocker spaniel named Peanut, was last seen a few blocks from Gran's house. No reward is offered and she's been missing for almost a week. But she might have been found by now, so I ask Gran if I can use her phone.

When I call, there's no answer. Drats.

Since I'm in an investigating mood, I pull out all the missing pet papers. Becca already called most of the owners but some didn't answer. Once I know which pets are still missing, I'll bike around looking for them.

I carry Gran's phone and a bag of wheat chips into the living room, and I curl up on the couch with the papers. I hear Gran's computer clicking from her home office and know she'll be busy for a while.

Who should I call first? I ponder, flipping through the flyers.

Let's start at the beginning—A for Ali Baba, a labrador retriever missing for eight days. No reward offered. I'm starting to think it's no coincidence that the pets with owners offering rewards are returned quickly. But those without rewards...I'm afraid for them.

I'm more determined than ever to stop the pet-nappers.

I call Ali Baba's owner but after five rings I get an answering machine: *Hi. This is Tina. Sorry I can't answer. Leave your number after the beep.*

What number should I give? Last time we made calls, we left Leo's number. But I can't leave Gran's number because I'll be gone in a few hours. And if I leave my home phone, someone else in my family will probably answer. It could be complicated. So I hang up.

Next I call about Miracle, a cute silky terrier with purple toenails and a rhinestone purple collar. A man tells me the dog is still missing.

"I'm sorry," I say. "I'll be on the lookout for him."

"Don't look too hard." He snorts like this is a hilarious joke. "It's my wife's dog and it's been peaceful around here without it yapping all the time. She wanted to offer a reward, but I'm not paying to get that stupid dog back."

When he hangs up, I scowl and mutter, "Jerk," and vow to look extra hard for Miracle.

I flip through the flyers until a photo of a calico cat named Violet stops me.

Her sweet multicolored face and topaz eyes

remind me of Leo's kitten. I sigh. Not his kitten anymore. By now Honey, Chris, and No-Name are with a foster family...

I press my lips tight.

Do. Not. Think. About. Kittens.

I put the flyer down...then pick it up again. Why is Violet so familiar? I've biked all around town lately but don't remember seeing her.

I read the details. Violet was lost a few blocks from Helen Corning Middle School, so I may have seen her on my way to school. I check the date she went missing — almost two months ago. If she hadn't been returned by now, it's unlikely she ever will.

I read through details: Female calico, two years old, crooked right ear, no collar, and when she went missing she was expecting kittens...

OMG!

I look closer at Violet. Her long black whiskers curl like Becca's kitten; her coloring is like Leo's kitten, and she has topaz eyes like my sweet Honey.

No wonder she reminds me of our kittens.

She's their mother.

- Chapter 20 -
Follow That Pet-Napper

I grab the phone, my heart racing as I punch in the number from the flyer.

One ring, two, three...seven, eight.

A recording invites me to leave a message, and this time I do. "Hi, I'm Kelsey," I say in a rush. "I'm calling about your cat. Please call back—it's important!" I leave Gran's number.

"Hurry! Call back!" I whisper to the phone.

The phone ignores me.

Maybe I should have left my home number too. I could call again to leave it...No, I'll just wait. Even thought it's so hard. Dad will be finished volunteering at Veteran's Hall and here to pick me up in an hour. If she doesn't call back before then,

I'll call later from home. I *have* to talk with her.

Five minutes pass. I cross my legs then uncross them. I eat a few chips then toss the bag aside. I grab it again and reach in for another handful of chips.

When I grow tired of staring at the phone, I pick up my mystery novel where I left off and read.

After a few paragraphs, though, I start to wonder about Violet. Her owner must be heartbroken, not only missing a cat but wondering if she had kittens. I can assure her that the kittens are safe but I don't know where Mama Cat is—and I'm scared to guess what happened to her.

The phone rings.

I grab it so fast, the chip bag spills to the carpet.

"Hi!" I say excitedly into the phone.

"Um...hello. Did you just call me?" The caller sounds younger than my mom, probably in her twenties.

"Yes, I did!" I exhale a sigh of relief. "I got your number from your missing pet flyer."

"Oh, well, that explains it." She laughs. "Only you're a little late."

"Late?" I tighten my grip on the phone.

"A wonderful man just called to say he found my dog!" Her voice rises with excitement. "I'm so thrilled I can hardly think straight. I've been in a state of terror for days but now that's over. I can't wait to see my sweet Ali! The man who found him is on his way right now."

"I'm so happy for you." My brain backs up and replays. "Wait—did you say *dog*? But I thought you were missing a female cat."

"Wrong on both counts—Ali Baba is a male lab. But you should already know that because you called me first."

"Well yeah." I check my notes and find Ali Baba's name with a notation, No answer. But I didn't leave my number. Of course most phones have caller ID and show missed calls. Mystery solved.

"I was calling to see if your dog is still missing," I say awkwardly. "I'm glad he was found."

"Thank you! I'm thrilled and a little giddy— it's like I have a date with my own dog. I have to find his favorite toy and fill his food bowl. Got to go!"

She clicks off, sounding so happy that I'm smiling too—until I realize my mistake. Palm smack to my forehead. Why didn't I ask her about the man who found Ali Baba? What if he has a spider tattoo or looks like Santa Claus?

I may have just missed my chance to catch a pet-napper.

Maybe it's not too late. If I hurry, I might be able to reach her house to see who will return the dog. I skim through the flyers until I find the one with a photo of a chocolate lab named Ali Baba.

I race into my grandmother's office and ask to use her computer to find an address. She moves aside, offering me her chair. A few key clicks and I have the address. It's less than two miles away.

"Gran, I need to meet a friend—ASAP," I say as I print out the map.

"Go ahead. Borrow one of my bikes, if you'd like."

"I hoped you'd say that." I hug her before heading to the garage.

Most grandparents would waste time with questions, like who my friend is and why I'm in such a hurry. But Gran Nola is cool. She says if I don't learn to make my own decisions now I never will. She also competes in competitive bicycle races so I have several bikes to choose from. I pick a metallic blue twenty-four-speed bike. It's a little big for me, but it's purple, my favorite color.

Wind tosses my hair as I pedal furiously past cars and houses, stopping only for traffic lights. The map flaps like a pale bird in my hand. At Wright Street, I'll make a left then a right and another left before I reach 1979 Marcola Street.

What will I do when I get there? How will I know if the dog has already been returned? Should I knock on the door and explain that I'm trying to catch a pet thief?

When I turn onto Marcola Street, the map leads me to an L-shaped blue house with a high hedge surrounding the front yard. A blue mini-van is in the driveway and a dented brown Toyota is parked on the street in front of the house. I wish I could see into the backyard but it's blocked by a high stone wall.

Now what do I do? I wonder. If Leo were here, he'd bravely climb the fence to snoop into the backyard. If Becca were here, she'd go boldly up to the front door and ask questions.

But I'm scared to climb into a strange yard, and talking to strangers makes me nervous. I ride my bike past the house, so slowly I might as well be going backward. It's a dead-end street, so when I reach the end, I turn around and bike past the blue house again. I can't just keep riding back and forth, but there aren't any willow trees to hide under.

So I hide in plain sight; a clever spy strategy I learned in *Surveillance Techniques and Strategies.* I stop two houses away across the street, and fiddle with my bike chain like it isn't working right.

As I wiggle the bike chain, my hair falls over my face and I study the blue house. No open curtains or activity outside. But what's happening inside? Has Ali Baba been returned or is the pet-napper on his way? All I can do is wait and watch. But after ten minutes, I'm tired of waiting.

It's time for bold action. I push my hair from my face and get ready to bike across the street. But the front door suddenly opens and a stocky man in a big western hat steps out of the blue house.

"Glad I could help, ma'am." His deep voice has a Texas twang that carries across street.

"You were so kind to bring him home," a middle-aged woman with black hair piled high on her head says. She follows the man down the porch steps, a chocolate-brown dog wagging his tail after her.

Ali Baba! I think excitedly.

The man moves toward the brown Toyota with a rolling stride like he spends more time on a horse than in a car. I look down when his gaze shifts over to me. I let my hair fall over my face again, a convenient camouflage for sneak-watching.

Don't act suspicious, I remind myself. *You're just a kid out riding and you're checking your bike chain.*

"I wish I could do more for you," the woman calls from the porch. "Thank you so much."

"I should be the one thanking you," he says humbly with a pat on his pocket—right where a man usually keeps his wallet.

"Money can't replace a family member." She pats the dog beside her. "It's wonderful having Ali Baba back."

"Mighty glad to help out, ma'am." A Texas-sized bunch of keys on a silver key chain jangles as he unlocks his car. He turns back to wave and I gasp at the web of spider tattoos trailing down his right arm.

He's part of the pet-napping ring—and he's driving away!

Hopping onto my bike, I follow that car.

I pedal faster than I ever have, maybe even faster than Gran Nola when she competed in that big race in France. I focus on the bright red frame around his license plate. When Tattooed-Guy slows to make a right turn, I read his license plate: 3UWG382. I repeat it over and over in my head since I don't have a pen or paper. What kind of spy am I? I should have thought this through.

The Toyota gains speed, leaving me in his exhaust. I choke on fumes and my chest burns. The car slows into another right turn, blending into busy traffic. I've lost him.

"Drats," I mutter. At least I know what he looks like and I have his license number. But I have no clue how to track him down.

I consider going back to the blue house and explain that Spider Tattoo Guy is a pet thief. But what if Ali Baba's owner doesn't believe me? She might even slam the door in my face.

No one would slam a door in Becca's face. And Leo would know ways to track someone down with a license plate number. I miss my friends.

Sighing, I turn my bike around and head back to Gran's.

Dad's waiting for me when I roll up the driveway. I put the bike back in the garage, hug Gran Nola and Handsome good-bye, then follow Dad out to the car. I'm surprised he's not mad that I wasn't here when he showed up, but he's whistling to himself—something he hasn't done since moving to the apartment.

"Have a nice bike ride?" he asks as he starts up the car.

"Um...yeah, I guess." I click on my seatbelt. "Sorry I took so long."

"Oh, I didn't mind. I always enjoy talking with Nola. She has a great idea for improving my cream croissants and she gave me a lead on a bakery job."

"She did?" Instantly my mood shifts to hopeful. "If you get it, we could leave the apartment and buy a new house where we can keep Handsome."

"Whoa, Kelsey." Dad tousles my hair. "I don't even have an interview yet. I'll find out on Monday. Keep your fingers crossed."

"I'll cross my fingers, my toes, and everything."

"Even your eyeballs?" he teases. "I'll call you Cross-Eyed Kelsey."

I groan but he just chuckles.

He's reversing out of the driveway when I hear a shout and look over to the porch where Gran Nola is waving her phone.

"Call for Kelsey," she hollers.

"I'll just be a sec," I tell Dad and hop out of the car.

"Who is it?" I ask Gran, taking the phone from her.

"She didn't say." Gran Nola shrugs. "All she told me was that she's returning your call about a calico cat."

- Chapter 21 -
Mysterious Mama Cat

"Hello," I say, pressing the phone to my ear. "I'm Kelsey." My heart pumps so fast I'm dizzy.

"You called about my cat?" an elderly woman asks in a suspicious tone.

"I found your lost cat flyer and recognized the cat. Well, not her exactly...but her kittens."

"What kittens?"

"Your cat...Violet's...kittens. I know where they are," I add, aware of Gran's curious look.

"There aren't any kittens," the woman states with such certainty that for a moment I'm not sure if I have the right cat. But I remember Violet's topaz eyes and know I'm not mistaken.

"I've seen them and they're supercute," I insist

in my kindest voice. When I tell her I think Violet is dead, it's going to be a shock for her. "There are three kittens and one of them looks just like Violet."

"Is this a new trick to con money from me?" she demands.

I reel back like I've been slapped. "I don't want anything from you."

"That's what the man said too, until he asked for a reward. He told me he had my cat and her kittens—but I knew he didn't have my sweet Violet. I didn't believe him when he said there were kittens and I don't believe you."

"But your cat was pregnant when she went missing," I point out. "She would have had her kittens by now."

"If she did, they were born dead because Violet showed up last week alone. And my cat would never desert her own kittens. Don't call me again."

The woman hangs up.

Gran has a questioning look when I hand her back the phone.

"Are you in some kind of trouble?" she asks, slipping her arm around me. "I won't interfere if you don't want me to, but I'm here for you."

"Thanks, Gran. But this isn't about me. A friend of mine found some kittens." Close enough to the truth. "And I thought they belonged to the woman on the phone but she doesn't agree."

"What do you think?" Gran Nola asks.

"I think the kittens are hers. But she doesn't believe me so I can't do anything about it."

"You and your friend will think of something," she says, giving me a hug.

Unlike my grandmother, Dad believes he should know everything about his kids.

"What was that all about?" Dad demands as I join him in the car.

I have secrets to keep so I tell him the short, mostly true story about trying to help a friend find the owner of some lost kittens. When I finish, he says he's proud of me for trying to help a friend. Then he goes back to whistling.

When we get to the apartment, I rush for the phone. I may not be in a club anymore but I need to let Leo and Becca know that Mama Cat is still alive—unless I have the wrong cat.

But the clues add up:

> The ages of the kittens fit.
> Violet was missing when they were born.
> She returned right before we found the kittens.
> Her topaz eyes are identical to Honey's eyes.

According to my calculations (as Leo would say), I'm 99.9% sure Violet is Mama Cat. Besides, this gives me a good reason to call Becca. Once we're talking, I'll apologize for telling Leo she kissed Skeet.

But then I think about the kittens and anger rises up again. How could Becca give them to strangers? She didn't just break up the CCSC—she broke her promise to keep our kittens a secret.

So I call Leo.

He answers right away but I can't hear what he's saying over the loud voices in the background.

"Leo, turn down the TV," I say, raising my voice.

"I can't…" I hear a door open then shut, and the background noises stop. "Is this better?" he asks.

"Yeah. What were you watching?"

"Actually, it wasn't the TV." A pause. "It's my parents."

There's something troubling about his tone. "Are you okay, Leo?"

"Yes, it's just hard to hear you when they're yelling, so I had to go into the closet to talk."

"Oh, Leo. I'm so sorry. My parents argue sometimes but then they make up and are closer afterward."

"Mine argue more than sometimes. They're like two objects with net electric charge that repel each other," Leo says. "That's why they work long hours—to avoid each other."

"But they're avoiding you too, which is just wrong," I say angrily. I understand even more why the CCSC meant so much to Leo.

"I'm used to it," Leo says sadly. "So, why did you call?"

I tell him about my day: finding out about Mama Cat, spying on Spider Tattoo Guy, and chasing after him on my bike.

"It's physically impossible to catch a car with a bike," Leo says. "But it's cool you tried."

"And now my leg muscles hurt. It was crazy to follow a car on a bike."

Leo laughs. "If that was on video, you'd get over a million hits."

"And die of humiliation. But I was able to get the license plate. Can you track down a name or address from a license plate?"

"Not without breaking all kinds of laws by hacking into the DMV." He pauses. "I'll look into it."

"And I'd like to look at your bird-drone photos again. I have a feeling there's a clue there I missed." I hesitate, trying to connect the thoughts bouncing around in my head. But the memory is like a bubble that's already popped.

"I'll email the photos since it's like a war zone here right now."

"Maybe you should come over here," I offer, feeling bad for him.

"I can't leave my parents alone or it could get ugly," Leo says like he's joking but I worry he's serious.

"Is there anything I can do for you?"

"You've already done it." I can hear a smile in his voice. "You called me."

I print out Leo's photos, and bring them to my room. I spread the aerial photos out on my desk. I'm like a giant looking down at a dollhouse world of tiny yards, roofs, patio furniture, cars, barbecues, sheds, and even a few people. *There's a clue in here*

somewhere, I think, tapping my fingers on the pile of photos. But I don't see anything unusual. What am I missing?

Since I'm trying to solve two mysteries, I make two lists in my notebook.

PET-NAPPING CLUES:

• There are at least three thieves in the pet-napping ring: Spider-Tattoo Guy, an old lady, and a Santa look-alike.
• 3UWG382 is the license number on the brown Toyota.
• Only pets with rewards are returned quickly.

CAT-DUMPER CLUES:

• Violet disappeared five weeks ago.
• Kittens were born four to five weeks ago.
• Violet returned a week ago.
• The kittens were found in dumpster a week ago.
• A man called wanting a reward for Violet and kittens.

I read through the list a few times, sorting through facts and suspicions. One event jumps out at me—the man asking for a reward for Violet. I have it under facts about the kittens but it would also fit under my list of pet-napper clues.

That's when it hits me—I don't have two separate mysteries.

I have one. And Mama Cat is the connection.

Piecing together my clues, I try to imagine what happened.

A man—who might be part of a ring of pet thieves—stole or found Mama Cat. He hoped for a reward but instead—surprise! A litter of kittens. The kittens were about four weeks old and healthy when we found them, so they hadn't been away from their mother for long. But why would pet thieves raise kittens instead of returning them? Or were they waiting for the owner to offer a big reward? Only Mama Cat found her way home.

"And the pet-nappers dumped the kittens," I mutter angrily.

I'm more determined than ever to track down the pet thieves.

Leo's photos are the key, I think as I flip through them again. I don't see anything unusual but the feeling of missing something is stronger than ever.

So I go over to my closet and pull down my spy pack. Unzipping a side compartment, I pull out my magnifying glass. Feeling a bit like Nancy Drew, I hold the glass over each photo, studying each object: flowers, a swimming pool, barbecues, swings, bikes, toys, ponds, cars, garages…wait a minute!

What's that black shadow?

Holding the photo in the light, I can clearly see the shadow is actually a black tarp. And it covers a large round object as big as a car. It *is* a car! Silver glints from a bumper peeking out below a brown dented trunk. I can't read the license plate but it's framed in bright red—like the Toyota I chased today.

Could it be the same car?

- Chapter 22 -
What Kelsey Found

I don't need to ask Leo who lives in that house. I've biked past it so many times I recognize the blue Honda in the driveway and the empty spot reserved for a white animal control truck.

But why is Spider Tattoo's car hidden in Officer Skeet's backyard? I can't think of an innocent explanation, only a terrible suspicion. Is Officer Skeet part of the pet-napping ring? An animal control officer knows all about missing pets. Officer Skeet's too nice to be a suspect. I'd rather suspect his no-good nephew.

Still, I can't be sure the brown car is the same one I followed.

There's only one way to find out—return to

Willow Rose Lane.

It's too late tonight, so I plan to go in the morning. And a smart sleuth knows it's safer to bring back-up, so I zip off an email to Leo.

Spying in the morning. Meet under our tree.

Leo will be excited when I tell him about the hidden getaway Toyota.

I should tell Becca too, but I'm sure she'll hang up if I try to call her. And if I email her, she'll probably delete it. And when she finds out I suspect *both* Skeet and his uncle, she'll really, really hate me. But she needs to know who owns the kittens. She may hang up, delete me, and post online that I'm her worst enemy ever. But I send an email to her anyway.

It's hard to sleep that night, ideas and clues racing through my mind. I dose off then wake up again after midnight. The next time I wake up it's almost two o'clock. Finally at five fifty, I give up on sleep. I have places to go and people to spy on—so I dress quickly and grab my spy pack.

My family always sleeps in on Sunday morning so there's no one to question me when I tiptoe down the hall wearing a black hoodie over a black

T-shirt and black jeans. I stop by the computer to check my email, fingers crossed there's one from Leo. But nope. I email him again, urging him to meet me soon.

A stakeout is more fun with friends.

The morning air is chilly and I shiver inside my hoodie. I unlock my bike from the rack outside our apartment then head toward Willow Rose Lane.

Dawn casts a grayish haze over the streets like I'm riding into a cloud. As I pedal, I think about the photo with the brown Toyota. Was it really the same car? The photo was taken from a distance so all I could see was a corner of a brown trunk, silver bumper, and a red-framed license plate. Did I leap to the wrong conclusion? Maybe because I dislike Skeet and want to prove he's guilty? Because with proof of his guilt, Becca would have to forgive me and admit I was right.

But what if I'm wrong?

I'll find out with the help of my spy pack.

The biggest problem will be getting close enough to see the license plate. I'll have to climb up on the fence and lean over really far. What if someone sees me on the fence? That's why I need Leo as a lookout.

Only when I reach the willow tree, no Leo.

I wait and wait and wait. Finally, I give up.

Leo isn't coming.

I'm on my own.

A blue Honda and county truck are parked in Officer Skeet's driveway. If I'm lucky he's still sleeping. I only need a quick look over the fence, then I'm out of there. Easy-peasy.

A porch light shines golden across the driveway and lawn. I don't see any lights from inside the house, so I hide my bike between the two vehicles on the driveway.

I scan the area to make sure no one is watching, then I creep over to the high wall surrounding the yard. It's formidable and the gate is locked. I'll need to climb on a section of wall that's covered with spiraling star jasmine vines to get a look at the license plate.

Getting a hold of the vines isn't easy. My hands scrape on the prickly branches that aren't sturdy enough to support my weight. I dig my feet into the vines, inching my way up. I grit my teeth to keep from crying out when a sharp branch jabs me. I don't let go, though, and cling to the branches. My foot slips and I start to fall, flowers spilling around me, one into my mouth that I spit out. I keep grasping at flowery vines, pushing up until I feel solid wood beneath my stinging hands.

I pull myself up to the top of the wall and see the tarp. A rope dangles from the bottom right corner of the tarp where it's come untied, revealing the gleam of a car bumper. There's no mistaking a rusty brown car with a dented bumper. Unfortunately, I can't see the license plate from here.

Must. Get. Closer.

I lean over the fence, my feet dangling in the air. Tiny white blossoms fly up into my face like a cloud of butterflies. When I inhale, a blossom sucks into my mouth. As I choke, my hands slip and I'm tumbling, down, down, *splat* on soft grass on the other side of the fence.

"Eww!" I spit out the blossom and jump to my feet.

Since I didn't choke to death and no one has caught me (yet), I might as well get a closer look at the car.

I peer under the tarp and catch a glimpse of the license plate: 3UWG382.

Yes! I was right! And now I have proof that Officer Skeet, a sworn protector of animals, is involved in a pet-napping ring. Still, it's hard to believe. Why would someone who entertains kids at hospitals and rescues trapped ducks steal pets? *It's all about the rewards*, I think sadly. How much money does a county employee make anyway? Not enough to stop him from taking advantage of desperate pet owners.

And it's not just Officer Skeet—he has to have at least three accomplices. He's the one who steals the pets. Or maybe he finds them while on the job. He's too well-known in Sun Flower to return the pets for rewards, so his accomplices must do it. But most of the rewards are under a hundred dollars. Split it four ways and it's probably not enough to pay for gas in a getaway car. The math of pet-napping doesn't add up. Am I missing some important clue?

Since I'm already in the yard, I unzip my spy pack and fit my cap-cam over my head. I pull back the tarp so I get clear shots of the Toyota. As I click photos, I wonder how the pet-napping ring works. Who does the getaway car belong to? And I don't see any missing pets in Officer Skeet's yard, so who hides them after they're stolen? Spider Tattoo, the old lady, or Santa?

And then I hear barking...

The sound is far away like it's from a neighbor's

house. I cup my ear, straining to hear. There it is again! A muffled bark, so faint it's more like a vibration than a clear sound; like listening to my own heartbeat.

I look around the backyard—past the koi fish pond to a garden shed in the corner. I don't remember the shed in the photo. It's long and has dark shuttered windows.

Shivers run up my spine.

Leave now! a voice in my head warns. But I can't forget the barking.

What if a stolen dog is in the shed?

I move cautiously toward the shed. *I'll be quick*, I tell myself. And I won't do anything dumb—well, dumber than sneaking out of my house, biking to a possible criminal's house, and snooping in his backyard.

Keeping low and hugging shadows, I creep forward. My spy pack slips down my shoulder, jabbing my arm. The pain makes me cry out and I almost turn back. But I keep going.

The shed is in the far right corner of the backyard. I press up against the fence so I blend in with shadows. I hope Officer Skeet doesn't look outside. As I near the shed, I'm shocked to realize it's almost as big as a garage. Shady oak trees hanging over the roof camouflaged it in the aerial photos.

As I expected, it's locked. I can't hear any noises from inside, but there's a suspicious dark odor that reminds me of the kennels at Wild Oaks Animal Sanctuary. When I spot a small dark blob on the cement step in front of the door, my worst suspicions are confirmed.

A pile of dog poo.

Evidence a dog was here.

Of course, the dog could belong to Officer Skeet.

I really, really should leave. But I stare at the door lock, itching to use the lock pick kit in my spy pack. I've never broken into a building before—it's so Nancy Drew. But I've practiced picking locks on doors, windows, and suitcases for years. Those were easy-peasy—this lock is heavy steel and a real challenge.

In other words: irresistible!

Picking a lock is all about listening and intuition. I check the size of the lock and choose a metal pick like a toothpick from my pack. I poke it inside the lock, jiggling around and listening hard for a click. I'm a little surprised when the lock falls open after only a few attempts.

When I open the door and peek inside, the musty animal smell is overwhelming, and I can hardly believe what I see.

They're here! Not one missing pet—but almost all of them!

The front of the shed is for garden tools but the back is crammed with pet carriers holding cats, dogs, and even rabbits. In the far back corner, there's a floor-to-ceiling wire cage big enough for a goat—like the one that went missing but was returned within hours.

But why are the animals so quiet? It's like walking into a tomb except for the tail wag thumps and barks from a labrador retriever inside a large carrier. I hold my breath as I check the other animals inside carriers…afraid of what I'll find. I breathe again when I see they're all sleeping.

They must be drugged, I think, furious.

Moving from carrier to carrier, I look through the front bars.

The silky terrier with a purple collar and purple toenails has to be the missing Miracle—the noisy dog according to the husband of the owner. Yet she's quietly curled in a ball, sleeping. I recognize more dogs and cats from the flyers, but there are several that don't match my missing pet lists. In total, there are eleven dogs, three cats, and a rabbit.

Okay, this is serious. I have to get out now.

I almost make it. I'm a few feet from the door, and my hand is outstretched, ready to grab the knob...but then the knob starts turning.

Someone is opening the door from the other side!

- Chapter 23 -
Guilty and Innocent

No way out.

I look around for a hiding place. There isn't enough room to hide behind the carriers and the large livestock pen is enclosed in wire that's easy to see through. There's a closet in the back of the shed, and I race toward it.

Inside I find shelves with wigs, hats, make-up, a long, white beard, scarves, and a wooden cane. On the other side clothes hang on a pole, including a white doctor's coat, a pleated black skirt, leather pants, a studded jacket, and black boots.

I squeeze in with the hanging clothes then shut the door just as a boy calls out, "Is someone in here?"

As quiet as a shadow, I hold my breath. I wrap my arms around myself and my heart thuds like thunder.

"Uncle Kip, are you in here?" he calls again.

OMG—it's Skeet! I've avoided being his target at school, but if he finds me here, I'm in big trouble.

At least Becca can't say I accused him unfairly. He is capital G-U-I-L-T-Y. But I'm too scared for triumph. If Skeet searches the room, he'll find me...

"Why did Uncle Kip leave the door open?" Skeet mutters.

A dog barks—the labrador that led me here.

"Hungry, fella?" Skeet says in a gentle tone. Paper rustles, probably a bag of dog food. "That's a good dog. You like that, don't you."

Skeet talks like someone who genuinely loves animals—which is confusing until I guess what he's doing. He must be giving the dog a sleeping drug with the food.

Waiting in the dark closet without even a crack of light is torture. I can't move because I might knock something over. Why is there such an odd collection of clothes and accessories in here anyway? I think back over the descriptions of the various pet-nappers, and match them with the objects in this closet: a cane for the old woman; black boots and red pants for Santa; and a western hat for Spider Tattoo Guy.

Only why store clothes in a shed? Doesn't the old woman need her cane? Why don't Santa and Spider Tattoo keep their clothes at their own homes? It doesn't make sense...or does it?

Suddenly footsteps pound my way. I jump and bump the cane. It rattles to the floor just as the closet door is yanked open.

Skeet's mouth drops open. "*You!*" he cries.

"Um...yeah. Hi, Skeet." I try to act like there's nothing strange about my hiding in a closet. I even force a smile to hide my fear.

"Why are you here, Kelly?" Burton Skeet demands, his red ponytail whipping behind him like a deadly snake.

"It's Kelsey," I say uneasily.

"How did you get in here? No one is allowed except me and my uncle."

"Oh, my mistake," I say almost cheerfully. "I'll just be leaving..."

"Not until I figure out what's going on." His stocky body is a wall blocking my escape. "I have to tell my uncle."

"Don't!" I shake my head. "Just let me leave and forget I was here."

"You're not going anywhere until I figure out what's going on." He grabs my arm and drags me out of the closet.

"I won't go with you." I struggle to break free but he's all muscle. "And you can't force me to stay—that would be kidnapping."

"You're the one who illegally broke into my uncle's shed. So I have to tell him, even though you're Becca's friend." His forehead furrows into a deep frown. "I don't want Becca to get mad."

"She'll get really, really, *really* mad at you if you don't let me leave."

"I know and that sucks," he says, rubbing his forehead like he's getting a headache. "Why were you in the closet? Are you a thief?"

"Me? A thief?" I roll my eyes. "You and your uncle stole these animals."

"Don't be stupid." Skeet glares at me. "My uncle fosters animals for the Humane Society. Everyone respects him and the mayor even gave him an award for heroism. He helps animals a lot."

"Helps himself to rewards," I accuse. "And you're helping him."

"Yeah, I'm helping him care for the animals when I have free time." Skeet nods proudly. "I exercise and feed them."

"And drug them," I say with an angry look at the lab who is now sleeping like the other animals. "You make me sick. I don't get why Becca or any girl could like someone as cruel as you."

"I'm not cruel!" he argues, balling his fists. "I'm saving their lives by keeping them quiet. Or the neighbors would complain and they'd be put to sleep permanently because there's no more room at the shelter. They don't stay here long anyway because my uncle is good at finding homes for them. He works hard to help animals—just like Becca's mom. When there's room at the shelter, the animals will go there to be adopted."

"Liar!" It's weird how anger makes me forget to be scared. "Your uncle only takes homeless pets to the shelters. He keeps the ones with rewards until his accomplices can collect the reward money."

"That's bull." Skeet lifts his arm like he's going to hit me then lowers his hand. "I promised Becca I'd watch my temper, and I'm trying hard. But you're wrong about my uncle. He's the kindest, greatest man I know and you better not say mean things about him."

"You're telling *me* not to be mean?" Now I do

laugh but it's shaky and probably sounds a little crazy. "You help him steal pets."

"He rescues abandoned and lost animals."

"Stolen animals," I accuse.

"You don't know what you're talking about."

"I do—and I can prove it." I point to the silky terrier sleeping in a small crate. "His name is Miracle and his owner has been looking for him for over a week. She left flyers at the shelter—but Miracle never made it there."

"My uncle would never do that."

I point to a Scottie. "That black dog is named Togo. He's been missing for almost two weeks."

"No way." Skeet's grip on my arm slips, and I jerk away, but he catches me quick like a lizard snapping up a fly.

"You're as guilty as your uncle," I rush on. "When he's arrested, you'll be in trouble too."

"Arrested?" He looks around the room like it's a cage and he's as trapped as the animals.

"He didn't just steal pets," I go on, hoping to scare him into letting me go. "He tried to kill innocent kittens by tossing them in the trash. They would have died if we hadn't rescued them."

"You mean the kittens are still alive?" Skeet

chokes out.

"No thanks to you!" I practically spit at him. "Becca wouldn't believe me when I told her you were guilty. But I was right. We saw you near the alley after they were dumped. You left them to die in the dumpster, didn't you?"

"Of course I did," he answers with no shame.

I stare at him, shocked that he'd admit to something so horrible.

"They had to die," he adds in a calm voice that chills me. "It's not like I wanted to kill them. I had to do it to protect the other animals. The mother cat died of rabies, and they were infected too."

"Who told you that?" I demand.

"My uncle. He told me to drown them but the dumpster was closer and easier. I felt bad for the kittens but rabid animals have to be destroyed."

I try to wrap my brain around his words. Does he really believe the kittens were rabid? Or is he just lying so I won't tell Becca. But if he's telling the truth, he's both guilty and innocent. That's an oxymoron I bet even Leo can't explain.

"The kittens are healthy," I insist. "Ask Becca— she'll tell you. All three kittens were doing great the last time I saw them. Definitely not rabid."

"But my uncle said…" Skeet's words trail off.

"Do you believe everything he says? If you're telling the truth then he's lied to you to get you to do his dirty jobs. If they were rabid, why wouldn't he have them brought to the shelter to be euthanized?"

"He would never lie to me."

"Go ask him," I say, eager to get rid of him and escape.

"Yeah…I'll ask him." He blinks fast, his shocked eyes unfocused. "That's what I'll do. Right now."

I'm ready to run past him and out the open door. But his fingers dig into my skin and he drags me over to the goat cage. "You're not leaving—not until I know what's going on."

"Let go!" I try to break free of his steel-tight grip but he's too strong.

"And I'll take this," he adds, lifting my spy pack from my shoulders and tossing it to the floor. "So you can't use your cell phone."

He shoves me into the cage before I can tell him I can't afford my own cell phone.

Then he slams the cage door shut.

And locks it.

- Chapter 24 -
Caged

I rattle the lock—one of those combination locks like on a school locker—but it won't open.

And my spy pack, with my lock picks inside, is on the other side of the door—out of reach. *Think, Kelsey!* I urge myself. *And think fast because when Skeet comes back with his uncle I'll really be in trouble.*

I know too much for them to let me go.

Escape. There has to be a way out. Desperately, I look around the cage. It's about four-by-four; big enough for a goat, pig, or snoopy girl. The floor is covered with loose hay and tufts of fur. The wire is strong like steel. I'd need wire cutters to break out—which I have in my spy pack.

Pressing against the wire, I squeeze my arm through the biggest gap I can find but I can't reach far enough to grab my pack. I only end up with painful scrapes. There has to be a way out of here! I drop to the floor and search through the hay. I find tiny dark pellets (goat food or goat poop?), a broken black dog collar, and a rope about two feet long that probably bound the hay bale.

Rope! I think excitedly. I can use it to get my backpack.

But I'll need something to tie to the end of the rope—like a hook to grab my backpack. I peer through the wire and see a really big hay hook about three feet away. So I come up with the idea to use the rope to lasso the hay hook and tie the hook to the rope and catch my spy pack.

I tie a loop at the end of the rope, push my hand with the rope through a gap and throw the rope as far as I can.

Not only do I miss, but I see the rope isn't long enough.

Hopeless, I think as I sink to the floor.

Crying seems like a good idea and very tempting. But the Skeets will be back soon. How far will Officer Skeet go to avoid jail?

I don't want to stick around to find out.

The rope lasso idea might work if I can add more length to the rope. So I dig into the hay on the floor, searching for more rope. I don't find any but I pick up the broken dog collar. It's about a foot long with a metal buckle on one end. I stare down at the worn collar then at the rope. Neither is long enough to reach the hay hook separately, but what if I put them together?

Looping the rope through the hoop on the collar, I pull and tug to test the strength. Yes, this may just work!

I reach through the gap again and throw the rope-collar at the hay hook. Close, but another fail. I need to hook the metal loop on the collar over the pointed metal tip of the hay hook. Not easy, I find out after about twenty tries. But I loop the hay hook once before it slips off, so I know it's possible.

I feel like I've been trapped here for hours but it's probably only been ten minutes. Still, time is running out.

The Skeets will return soon.

Fear pushes me to try again and again and again. Sway, swing, throw, miss, then pull the rope back and start over. I've probably tried a million times when the collar-rope sails through the air and snags the hay hook.

It worked! Wow! It actually worked.

Carefully, I pull the rope toward me. It tugs at first because the hay hook is heavy. But slowly it scrapes across the floor. When the steel hook is close enough to reach, I pull it into the cage. Now all I have to do is tie the rope to the hay hook and swing it out to grab my spy pack. It seems impossible but so did getting the hay hook and now I'm holding it.

So I do the whole swing-throw-and-aim thing again. But it's harder with such a heavy weight on the rope.

It takes four tries before the steel hook snags my backpack strap.

I tug and pull and my spy pack moves an inch. Another inch. And another. I'm reaching for the spy pack when I hear footsteps from outside the door.

And the knob begins to turn...

- Chapter 25 -
Rescue

I freeze in place, my arm stretched through the wire, my fingers brushing against my spy pack. This can *not* be happening. Not when I'm so close to escaping. Drats!

The door inches open…

The Skeets are back and I'm still locked up. I've never felt so helpless in my life. What's going to happen to me? Officer Skeet can't let me go because I know about his crimes and he'll end up jailed in a cell not much bigger than this cage. If I promise not to tell anyone, maybe he'll let me go. He's a pet-napper, not a kidnapper, so he won't hurt me, I hope. But keeping his crimes secret would be wrong. More pets would be hurt. What am I going to do?

I'm shaking as I clutch the hay hook in my hand, ready to use the sharp weapon to save my life.

The door opens wider. I see a polished brown shoe and...

"Kelsey," a voice calls out. "Are you in here?"

"Leo?" I exclaim in disbelief.

He steps into the room, light from outside glints off his blond hair like he's part angel. I'm so happy to see him I feel like singing, "Hallelujah!"

"I'm here!" I jump to my feet, the hay hook thudding to the hay-covered cement. "I'm so glad it's you! When that door opened I thought you were Skeet!"

"I look nothing like him." Leo tilts his head, puzzled. "I'm much smaller and shorter."

"I didn't mean *really* him—just that he's coming back and bringing his uncle—who I so do not want to see. Hurry, get me out of here!"

"Why are you in a cage?"

"Really?" I roll my eyes. "That's the question you ask me?"

"It's a logical question."

"You think being in here was my idea?"

"No." He jiggles the cage door. "It's locked."

"Great deduction, Sherlock." My words are

sarcastic but I'm smiling because I'm so glad here's here. "How did you know I was in trouble?"

"I found your bike but not you. So I flew my bird-drone over the yard and when it came back the camera showed Burt Skeet leaving the shed and looking meaner than usual."

"I think he was more scared than mean," I say.

"I was scared when I couldn't find you," Leo admits. "Sorry I wasn't here sooner. I didn't check email until after breakfast."

"It's okay. You're here now."

He looks nervously around the shed. "These animals are unnaturally quiet. Are they dead?"

"Not dead—drugged by Officer Skeet." I glance at the door nervously. "No time for explanations, we can do more for the animals once we get away. I don't want to be here when Officer Skeet shows up. He fooled everyone. But he won't anymore if I can get out of here."

Leo jiggles the lock. "Where's the key?"

"No idea. But I have picks in my spy pack. Be quick—unless you want to deal with two Skeets."

Leo goes pale but moves quickly. He digs into my spy pack for the picks. He jabs the lock a few times but it won't open. So he slips the picks through the cage to me and holds the lock sideways so I can jiggle the pick in the tiny hole. The sweetest sound in the world is the lock clicking open.

When Leo opens the cage door, I tumble out, falling against him. He grabs and holds me in his arms so I won't fall. While I catch my breath, I lean against him like we're hugging. We both jump back from each other.

"Thanks," I say, pretty sure I'm blushing because he is too.

He just nods, looking down at his shoes.

"Let's get out of here." I'm already opening the door. When I step outside, the gray clouds have cleared to a sky bright with sunshine and I take a wonderful deep breath that tastes like freedom.

Leo and I race across the yard, past rainbow koi fish swimming in a pond and a car half-hidden under a tarp. He offers me a boost to the fence, and climbs up beside me. We're poised to jump down when there's a shout.

It's the Skeets—both of them.

Burt Skeet's red ponytail flies behind him as he runs toward us shouting, "Stop!"

Behind him, Officer Skeet is running toward us too.

"You kids get back here!" he shouts with the fierceness of a man who is used to giving orders.

"Not a chance," Leo says, balancing on top of the fence beside me.

When Leo offers me his hand, I take it and we both jump to the other side of the fence.

Safe.

I don't find out that Becca was partly responsible for my escape until we're far enough away from the Skeet house to rest in a busy grocery store parking lot. Leo stops his gyro board and I coast up beside him. He takes out his cell phone and I watch over his shoulder as he texts Becca: *She's ok*.

That's when I find out what happened. When Leo got to the willow tree and I wasn't there, he rode around until he spotted my bike hidden by the Animal Control truck. When he couldn't find me, he called Becca. He told her all about our suspicions about Officer Skeet and his nephew.

"She believed me," Leo says. "Then she told her mother—who got in touch with her friend Sheriff Fischer—who headed right over to the Skeet house.

While I waited for him, I heard voices from the backyard and my bird-drone took the picture of Burt Skeet leaving the shed. I decided there wasn't time to wait for the sheriff. I sent a text to Becca, saying I was going in after you."

"And you found me," I say. "That was really brave."

He shakes his head. "According to my calculations, there was only .28 percentage of danger. If I hadn't helped you, the sheriff would have. He's probably already arrested Officer Skeet."

"I hope so, although..." I think of Burt Skeet. I believe he really didn't know his uncle was a pet-napper. He may have a strong streak of meanness toward short kids but he really admires his uncle.

Leo is hopping on his gyro-board, so I climb back onto my bike. I expect him to turn off for his own house but he stays with me all the way home.

When I invite him in, he shakes his head. "I just wanted to make sure you got home okay."

"I'm okay." *Thanks to you*, I think. But I don't want to embarrass him.

"Uh...I better go. My parents were acting weird— weirder than usual—when I left. They were talking without yelling."

"That's a good thing," I say.

"Maybe." He brushes dirt off his shirt. "They want to have a family meeting."

He zooms off as I walk up the steps into my apartment—where my family is still sleeping. The wall clock shows it's been only an hour and a half since I left home. Unbelievable!

I should wake up my parents and tell them everything but my legs wobble like noodles and I'm so tired I go straight to my room. I drop my spy pack on the floor, climb into bed, and fall asleep.

- Chapter 26 -

Interrogated

"Kelsey, Kelsey!"

My mother's voice breaks through a deep fog of sleep. I open one eye and then the other. "Huh?" I murmur, not sure why I've been sleeping when the sun is shining like it's late afternoon.

Mom holds out the phone and looks at me with the strangest expression ever. "Kelsey, why is Sheriff Fischer calling to speak to you?"

Instantly, I'm awake.

"Oh…that." I take the phone and sit up straight in bed. I look down at the black spy clothes I'm still wearing, and everything rushes back.

This begins a confusing afternoon of questions and answers and shocked looks from my family.

Usually I'm the one snooping outside doors, but during my long explanation to the sheriff, I catch Kenya and even Kyle listening in the hall.

I answer Sheriff Fischer's questions honestly but I don't tell him about the kittens, the Skunk Shack, the CCSC, and even Burton Skeet. I skip the part about him locking me in a cage. I guess I feel sorry for him. Weird, huh?

I'm a collector of secrets, so I give the sheriff a short version. I tell him that Becca, Leo, and I noticed a lot of pet disappearances. Our suspicions grew when we found out the same tattooed man had returned several dogs for rewards. And I give Leo the credit for taking aerial photos that led to the discovery of the brown Toyota in Officer Skeet's yard. I say I knew it was wrong to go into the shed but I heard barking and worried a dog needed help.

I finish by telling Sheriff Fischer that I took photos and lists of information we collected about the missing pets.

The sheriff says he has more people to talk to and that my parents may need to bring me to the station.

"I'll need more information on this pet thieving ring," he adds, and I hear paper rustling like he's consulting his notes.

"Sure. But I never saw the old lady or the Santa look-alike. I only saw the man with the Spider Tattoos."

"Tell me everything you can remember about him," Officer Skeet says.

"He wore a western hat and boots, and he carried a big silver key ring." As I say this, something clicks in my head. I think back to when I pedaled after Spider Tattoo to hiding out in the closet in Officer Skeet's shed.

And a crazy idea hits me.

"You say there are four people involved in the pet-napping ring?" Sheriff Fischer is asking. "Skeet, two men, and an elderly woman. One man has a spider tattoo and the other has a white beard like Santa. Is that right?"

"That's right...but it's wrong too." I can just imagine Leo saying nothing can be both wrong and right. But it's the truth, and the more I add up the clues, the more I know I'm right.

When I explain to the sheriff what I think really happened, he seems surprised but glad too.

"You just made my job easier," he says with a chuckle then hangs up.

I'm returning the phone to its cradle when my

parents come for me. They take me to their room and do some interrogating of their own. I give the same story I gave the sheriff; short and truthful, minus a few spying details that would get me grounded for life.

"You shouldn't have gone into a stranger's yard," Mom says sternly, but her arm is around me and she doesn't sound mad.

"I thought an animal was hurt," I say. "And he wasn't a stranger. I met him when I was at Becca's house."

"Just don't do it again," Dad adds, giving me a hug too.

Then we do something my family hasn't done since Dad lost his job—we go out to dinner. All six of us dine at a nice restaurant with cloth napkins. No plastic silverware or fast food.

Everyone is in a great mood. Dad is excited about his job interview tomorrow. Mom is confident Dad will get this job. My brother tells us all (in boring details) about a college he's applying to which offers a full-ride scholarship. Even my sisters are interested to hear about my adventure this morning.

I have a great time, ordering a cheeseburger

dripping with cheese and my favorite zucchini fries. Dad even lets us have ice cream for dessert.

But all through the fun, I wonder what's happening with Leo, Becca, the missing animals and the Skeets. How did Leo's family meeting go? Since Becca was involved in my rescue, does that mean we're friends again? Will all the animals be returned to their owners? And what happened to the Skeets?

If Officer Skeet is locked up in jail, he'll find out how it feels to be caged like an animal. I'm proud that I helped stop him stealing any more pets.

It's not until the next day that I find out what really happened.

- Chapter 27 -
A Little Bit of Justice

I wake up the next morning thinking of kittens...
and missing my Honey. I wonder where she's
living now. Is she close by or on the other side of
town? Is she in kitty foster care or adopted into
a family?

If only I could adopt her. I'd sleep with her every
night so when I wake up she'd be curled up beside
me. But even if Dad gets this job, it'll be months
before we can move into a house. By then Honey
will have forgotten about me. But I'll never ever
forget about her.

You'd think that after all the drama yesterday,
I'd be allowed to stay home from school. But not
even. My parents are annoying that way.

I don't mind going to school, though, because I have so much to ask Leo and Becca. I want to know what they told the Sheriff and if they've heard anything new. There hasn't been any news on TV or online about Officer Skeet's arrest—and I'm going crazy with curiosity.

At school, when I finally spot Becca, she's with the Sparklers. I start to walk over to her, but she sees me and turns away from her friend to mouth to me, "See you after school. Skunk Shack." She turns back to talk to her friends.

Really? I think with a rush of anger. After everything we've been though, she's still pretending not to know me? Well, I'll show her—I'll ignore her in homeroom. Even if she turns around to talk to me, I won't reply. I won't meet her after school at the Skunk Shack. I won't ever talk to her again. I have other friends. I do *not* need Becca Morales.

Leo will talk to me, I have no doubt of that.

But Leo isn't at school.

So at lunch I sit at my usual table with Ann Marie and Tori. I try not to listen to Becca's laughter from two tables away. She's with her real friends, I remind myself. I. Do. Not. Care.

It's like the last week never happened. No Leo or Becca, no kittens, no club. I don't want to feel sorry for myself, but someone has to and I'm very good at self-pity. I don't wallow long, though, because of the rumors.

Leo isn't the only one missing school—Burton Skeet is also absent. And rumors about him fly like feathers in a twister. Some say he's at juvenile hall while others say he's moving away with his uncle. I don't know exactly why he's gone, but I know more than the other kids. Poor Skeet.

I doubt he's changed into someone who will be kind and never squish a short kid in a locker. But I understand the pain of losing faith in someone you admire. I've never told anyone but I used to look up to my dad like he was a superhero. If I broke something, he fixed it. If I cried, his strong hugs held me together. And when my siblings wouldn't play with me, he'd challenge me to a game of chess. There was nothing he couldn't do—until he lost his job and confidence. He became less hero and more human. I still love and respect him—just in a more realistic way.

Burton is dealing with a whole lot of reality.

The rumors, unfortunately, only confuse the

facts. By the end of school, I have no idea what happened to either of the Skeets.

But I'm pretty sure Becca knows, so I swallow my anger, and bike to the Skunk Shack.

When I get there, Becca is sitting outside on a stump, still wearing the tiger-striped skirt and shimmery gold blouse from school. She didn't stop by her house to change her clothes.

"I won't stay long," I tell her with my chin held high.

"I wish you would," Becca says softly. "Please don't be mad at me."

"Me? Mad at you?" I shake my head. "You're the one mad at me. You ended our club—remember?"

"About that..." Her dark curls droop around her face as she glances down at the weedy ground. "I'm always telling Burt to control his temper but I need to do it too. I'm sorry."

"I'm sorry too," I say. "I shouldn't have told Leo you kissed Burt."

"Yeah, you shouldn't have. But I did stuff I shouldn't have either—including that stupid kiss." She makes a bitter face. "I can't believe I thought he was a nice guy. He was working with his crooked uncle all this time and I think he tossed the kittens in the dumpster. I was so wrong about Burt, and you were right."

"Not that right," I say and tell her about Burt's uncle convincing him the kittens were rabid.

"He could have told his uncle no," Becca argues.

"It's not easy refusing someone you admire."

"You're defending him to me?" Becca asks, surprised.

I give her a faint smile. "I still don't like him."

"I don't either...but I did." Becca rubs her finger on a knotty hole in the stump she's sitting on. "The other Sparklers thought we'd make a cute couple so they kept pushing me to go out with him. I finally did—just to a movie. I even had a good time. But it doesn't matter anymore because you were right—he's a jerk. And I'm glad he's gone."

"Where is he?" I suck in my breath. "Jail?"

"So you heard that rumor too." She chuckles. "But it's wrong. Burt sent me an email saying good-bye and that he's sorry. His dad doesn't want him influenced by his uncle, so he's moving in with his dad in Chicago."

"But his uncle won't be around because he'll be in jail," I say.

"No. He wasn't arrested and may not ever be." Becca frowns, brushing off an ant crawling on her skirt. "The laws protecting animals aren't the same as for people. Mom is spitting mad and says she'll make sure he never works in this county again."

"But weren't all the stolen animals in his shed enough proof?" I ask.

"Minor charges like animal cruelty are rarely enough for jail. He told the Sheriff he was trying to protect the animals from the real pet-nappers and blamed everything on his accomplices."

"Sheriff Fischer wouldn't believe that," I say with certainty.

"Yeah, he didn't. But how did you know?"

I smile because this is a secret I can share. "I know because there are no accomplices."

"Yes, there are," Becca insists, standing up to face me. "Leo told me you spied on the guy with the spider tattoo."

"I chased him too—on my bike."

"Really?" Becca laughs. "But a bike can't chase a car."

"I figured that out the hard way," I say, holding up my callused hands. "But it wasn't till later that I remembered the jumbo-sized silver key ring Spider

Tattoo carries—exactly like the one Officer Skeet has. And I remembered your saying Officer Skeet likes to dress up in costumes to entertain sick kids."

"Yeah," Becca says, nodding. "He used to perform in the local theater."

"He never stopped performing," I add with a shake of my head. "I didn't connect it all until after I was hiding in the shed closet and found costumes and props like the cane for the old lady, Santa's beard and black boots, and the western hat for Spider Tattoo Guy."

"You mean the entire pet-napping ring was just one person?" Becca's mouth falls open.

I nod. "Officer Skeet in costumes."

"I guess it makes sense," she says after a moment. "County officials can't collect rewards for doing their job. So he collected the rewards in costumes so dramatic no one looked closely at his face. He may not go to jail, but he was fired from his job."

"It's a little bit of justice," I say, satisfied.

Becca moves toward the Skunk Shack door. "Let's go inside."

"What the point?" I swallow bitterness. "We don't have a club anymore."

"We can, if you want." Becca looks at me hopefully.

"But you gave the kittens away."

"Actually, I didn't even tell my mother about them." Becca smiles then pushes open the door.

I'm already rushing into the Skunk Shack—and there they are. Three tiny kittens curled together in their comfy kitty bed.

"Honey!" I cry, kneeling beside her.

Honey lifts her head to look at me with a meow as if to say, "Where have you been? I missed you."

At least that's what I imagine she's thinking when I scoop her up. And as I hold her close to my heart, she starts to purr.

When Leo joins us, he's just as shocked and delighted to see the kittens as I am.

As he hugs his calico kitten, he turns to Becca with a cautious expression. "Does this mean that we're in a club again?"

Becca and I share a smile and we both nod.

"Yes indeed," Becca tells Leo. "The CCSC is back in business. The cat-dumper case is solved but we still have to care for three kittens."

"Actually...only two," Leo says with a smile so tense it's more like a frown.

"I count three." I point to the kittens. "What are you talking about?"

He picks up his kitten and sits down at the table with her on his lap. "Remember that family meeting I had with my parents?"

"Sure." I nod. "How did it go?"

"Good and bad. Bad news is my parents are getting a divorce."

"Oh, Leo!" Becca cries, rushing over to put her arm around him. "I'm so sorry."

"Are you okay?" I ask but I don't touch him— not after that weird accidental hug we had when he rescued me from the cage.

"I'm very okay," he assures us. "It's easier than living in a war zone. There won't be any more fights and my parents will be happier living apart. Dad must have been planning this for a while because he already has an apartment and says I can stay with him whenever I want. He has a room for me in his new apartment."

"As long as you're okay," Becca says.

"I used to dread going home because of their fights. Now that they won't be avoiding each other, I'll probably see Dad more often. I'll miss living with Dad—but not his allergies." Leo pauses. "So I told Mom I wanted a cat—and she said yes."

"OMG!" Becca bounces up and down. "This is so amazing! You get to keep your kitten!"

He nods. "If it's okay with you."

"It's better than okay," she says, and I agree.

I'm super happy for Leo, but a little envious. I want to keep my kitten so much. But with the CCSC back together, I'll see her almost every day.

By the time we leave the Skunk Shack, Leo has named his kitten.

Lucky.

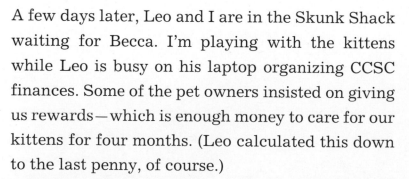

A few days later, Leo and I are in the Skunk Shack waiting for Becca. I'm playing with the kittens while Leo is busy on his laptop organizing CCSC finances. Some of the pet owners insisted on giving us rewards—which is enough money to care for our kittens for four months. (Leo calculated this down to the last penny, of course.)

There's a thud as the door bursts open and Becca comes rushing in. Her face is flushed and she's breathing hard like she ran the entire way from her house to the shack. The kittens, startled, duck underneath the grandfather clock.

"Is something wrong?" I ask, coming over to Becca.

"No. But I had to hurry through my chores before I could join you. And before I left I checked my email and got some info I've been waiting for."

"About what?" I ask.

"The kittens. I wanted to solve something on my own since you and Leo had a big adventure in Skeet's shed, and I felt left out."

"Being locked in a cage wasn't fun." I'm surprised that someone as popular as she is could ever feel left out. "Next time I'm locked in a cage, you can join me."

"No thanks," she says, laughing.

"So what was in the email?" I ask Becca.

"Since you and Leo found out *who* dumped the kittens, I did some online sleuthing and found out what happened *before* the kittens were dumped." Becca lifts her cell phone, its glittery pink case sparkling under the lamp. "I know where they were born."

Leo closes his laptop. "How did you find out?" he asks.

"By emailing an informant," she says mysteriously. "Mama Cat had our kittens in a barn off Murphy Road."

"That's not far from our school—where Violet was lost," I say, more sure than ever that Violet is our kittens' mother. Not that it matters now. The kittens are happy here.

"The farmer living there found the mother with her kittens in his barn," Becca continues. "The mother was catching mice, so he decided feeding her was a fair trade. But he mentioned the cats to a friend who told the animal control officer. Skeet recognized Mama Cat from a missing flyer and hoped to get a big reward for all four cats. So he went to the farmer disguised as a jolly fat man with a Santa beard and said the cats belonged to him. He took the cats home, but the mother ran away. So he was left with four-week-old kittens."

"I know he tried calling Violet's owner to get a reward," I say. "But Violet had already returned home and her owner wasn't interested in kittens. The woman accused Officer Skeet off conning her and told him never to call again."

"We know the rest of the story," Becca says sadly. "Officer Skeet didn't want to keep evidence of his crime, so he told his nephew the kittens were infected with rabies. Burt didn't want to kill them—he really does love animals—but he believed his uncle."

When Becca says this, I know who emailed her this information: Burton Skeet. I don't ask her about this though. She's allowed to have secrets of her own. It's not my business who she likes or dislikes. As long as she likes me enough to (hopefully) become my best friend.

Leo and I congratulate Becca on solving the final piece in the cat-napping mystery. One mystery solved by the CCSC.

But there are more, I think as I flip through my notebook for the list of three mysteries I made a week ago.

I put a check by the kitten-dumping mystery and write the word solved.

But that still leaves two mysteries—why a grandfather clock was left in the Skunk Shack and who owned the zorse.

I smile to myself because I like having a few unsolved mysteries to puzzle over. And it's great being in a club all about helping animals. We're going to keep looking for lost pets. One day a week we'll ride around, searching for missing animals. Not for any rewards, but because we want to help.

Right now I'm just having fun hanging out with my club mates. Leo has gone back to tinkering with the grandfather clock. It still doesn't work but it has shiny new parts. Becca is drawing a design for leopard spotted curtains for our clubhouse in her sketchbook. I'm doing what I love best—playing with my sweet Honey. I giggle when she chases a catnip mouse on a string.

Lucky spies a spider and chases after it. Honey abandons the toy mouse to chase after Lucky's tail. And Chris, who loves to sleep, snoozes curled up in the cat bed.

All three kittens jump when Becca's phone rings.

"It's Mom," Becca says.

Becca goes strangely quiet. Her eyes grow big and she gasps as she listens. When she hangs up, she looks positively stunned.

"What's wrong?" I ask, sitting down beside her at the table.

"I can hardly believe it," she says with a shake of her dark curls. "Mom told me she just had a call from a man in Nevada looking for his missing zorse. He's sure Zed belongs to him and he's coming here to take Zed home."

Leo's forehead creases. "Is this good or bad news?"

"I'm not sure..." Becca's words trail off, and I know exactly what she's thinking because I'm thinking the same thing.

I'm scared for Zed. What if his owner is the same person who scarred him so badly? We can't let him go back to an abusive owner. How can we find out what really happened to Zed?

Another mystery for the CCSC to solve.

I can't wait.

Stay tuned for the next Curious Cat Spy Club mystery!

Coming soon!

About the Author

At age eleven, Linda Joy Singleton and her best friend, Lori, created their own Curious Cat Spy Club. They even rescued three abandoned kittens. Linda was always writing as a kid—usually about animals and mysteries. She saved many of her stories and loves to share them with kids when she speaks at schools. She's now the author of over thirty-five books for kids and teens, including YALSA-honored The Seer series and the Dead Girl trilogy. Her first picture book, *Snow Dog, Sand Dog*, was published by Albert Whitman & Company in 2014. She lives with her husband, David, in the northern California foothills on twenty-eight acres surrounded by a menagerie of animals—horses, peacocks, dogs, and (of course) cats. For photos, contests, and more check out www.LindaJoySingleton.com.

The Mystery
- of the -
Zorse's Mask

A mysterious stranger has come forward as the owner of Becca's beloved zorse, Zed. But something seems suspicious about his claim. If this person is Zed's real owner, the Curious Cat Spy Club also fears he might be the one responsible for abusing Zed in the past. Kelsey, Becca, and Leo are determined to uncover the truth before they have to give him up. Maybe some sleuthing will dig up the dirt on this suspect. But when a daring rescue attempt puts Kelsey in danger, does the CCSC have enough spy skills to save her? Or are they in over their heads?